CHINHOMINEY'S SECRET

Bridge Works Publishing Company
Bridgehampton, New York

Nancy Kim

a novel

Published in the United States by Bridge Works Publishing Company, Bridgehampton, New York. Distributed in the United States by National Book Network, Lanham, Maryland.

FIRST EDITION

The characters and events in this book are fictitious. Any similarity to actual persons, living or dead, is coincidental and not intended by the author.

Library of Congress Cataloging-in-Publication Data

Kim, Nancy, 1966–
    Chinhominey's secret : a novel / Nancy Kim. — 1st ed.
        p.   cm.
    ISBN 1-882593-28-6 (hardcover)
    1. Korean Americans — Fiction.   I. Title.
PS3561.I4144C48   1999
813'.54 — dc21   98-43999
                                                          CIP

10   9   8   7   6   5   4   3   2   1

Book and jacket design/illustration by Eva Auchincloss

PRINTED IN THE UNITED STATES OF AMERICA

To Seth

With much gratitude to Yeun Soo and Mi Wha Kim, David Desmond, Stephen Beke and Barbara Silberbusch for their support, encouragement and assistance during the writing of this book.

With great appreciation to Barbara and Warren Phillips and Stacey Donovan at Bridge Works for their advice, guidance and editorial expertise.

And of course, special thanks to Seth Burns, for so much patience, love and understanding.

Part I

Prologue

The old woman looked away, turning her gnarled face to the ceiling.

"What's the matter?" the visitor asked, "What have you seen?"

The old woman shook her head, as though the vision were too horrible to reveal.

"Tell me. What do you know? What have you seen?" the visitor pleaded.

The old woman took a deep breath, still refusing to look her visitor in the eyes. She replied, "He cannot."

"What do you mean?"

"Your son. He cannot marry this woman."

"But why?"

"Heartache," the old woman said, "He will have nothing but heartache. From one generation to the next. From one day to the next." She paused for a long moment, and then added, "He will have two children."

"Two children hardly sounds like heartache. More like headache," the visitor said with relief.

"Both girls. The first a blessing. She will bring nothing but happiness to everyone around her."

The visitor smiled.

"And the second?"

"The second a curse."

The smile disappeared.

"A curse?"

"Her destiny is linked to yours."

"What do you mean?"

"She will die young. She will die because of you. She will die before her own mother!"

"Nonsense!" the visitor said. She stood up quickly, knocking over one of the tea cups filled with green tea.

The old woman leaned back in her chair and closed her eyes. The visitor stormed out of the room, slamming the door behind her. After she left, the old woman opened first one eye, and then the other. She reached across the table for the stack of bills that was payment for today's session.

"She'll be back," the old woman thought with a smile, as she started to count the money.

The ones with bad fortunes always came back. Hope made them return.

Chapter 1

Myung Hee Choi has not seen her mother-in-law since she and her husband Yung Chul left Korea for the United States 22 years ago. They brought nothing with them but three suitcases, heads full of dreams, and hearts full of hope. Myung Hee had a dress custom made for the occasion — gold sleeveless silk with silver embroidery along the hemline. They were moving to Los Angeles, a mythical place where the sun always shone, movie stars drove around in convertibles and anybody could swim in the ocean.

She boarded the plane that would take them to the United States, holding her two-year-old baby girl in her arms, her husband following closely behind her. Never once did she question the rightness of her decision. She had the utmost confidence in Yung Chul, knew that he would take care of her and their two children, the one she held in her arms, and the one she carried in her stomach. But as she climbed the steps of the Pan Am aircraft in her gold silk dress, the wind whipping her hair about, she hesitated. Her husband placed one hand on his beautiful wife's shoulder and asked gently, *"What is the matter?"* Myung Hee didn't turn around, afraid that her gentle loving husband, so brave and full of adventure, would misinterpret the fear in her eyes. For it wasn't the fear of the unknown that stopped her, it was the fear of what she already knew, of what she was afraid she wouldn't be able to forget. Her mother-in-law's words still rang in her ears: *Your marriage is doomed.*

Yung Chul kept his hand on her shoulder, his fingers soft as a whisper, not pushing yet not pulling away. For a brief moment, the couple stood frozen, unable to move forward, unwilling to go back. Then Myung Hee felt a movement from her womb, powerful in its fluidity, surprising in its intimacy, and she was reminded of what she was doing and why. She looked down and into the face of her little daughter who, feeling the movement in her mother's belly, smiled up at Myung Hee with the secret knowledge of babies. Myung Hee glanced over her shoulder at her husband, who was still waiting patiently, anxiously, his eyes searching hers for an indication of what she wanted, what she might need, what he could possibly do to encourage her. Myung Hee lowered her eyes demurely, the corners of her full lips curving upward with pleasure, her smooth soft cheeks now rosy with pride. She turned and with determination climbed the remaining steps into the plane.

Myung Hee shakes the memory out of her head as briskly as she shakes the pillows into their cases, but she can't keep from wondering what her mother-in-law will think when she sees them again after so many years. What will she think of their modest three bedroom stucco house on a quiet, tree-lined street in West Los Angeles? Will she wonder why they don't live in a Beverly Hills mansion with a swimming pool? What will she think of their three cars, a Lexus, a Ford, and a Honda? Will she be impressed, or will she wonder why they don't have a Mercedes, a BMW, and a Porsche? Will she think they had made the right decision in coming here, to the land of opportunity? Or will her visit confirm her belief that the Fortune Teller was right?

"When your mother comes, I hope she doesn't expect me to entertain her all by myself," Myung Hee tells her husband.

"Don't worry. She would not want you to."

Myung Hee looks at her husband out of the corner of her eye, but his face reveals nothing. There is no tenderness there. His face is impassive, as though he were discussing the weather with a stranger in an elevator.

"Do you find it strange that she is coming to visit now, after all this time?" she asks. "It is more than twenty years."

Yung Chul looks at the carpet before responding, each word spoken deliberately, carefully, "She said only that it was time that she come. She wants to see her granddaughters."

"Both of them?" Myung Hee asks, her voice rising sharply. Yung Chul lifts his head, looking his wife in the face. "Things change. People can change."

His wife turns her head away and plumps the pillows silently.

Yung Chul, dressed in a gray pinstriped suit, picks up his briefcase and heads for the door.

"Before you go," Myung Hee says, "Help me move the bed."

"Move the bed?" he sighs. "But my back won't allow me to lift such heavy objects."

She rolls her eyes. "It allows you to play eighteen holes of golf without problem."

"Wife, don't criticize me about the one thing that gives

me a little pleasure. You can't expect me to sit at my desk every day."

"Okay. Forget it then. Your mother will have to sleep with her head pointing north."

Yung Chul sighs and puts his briefcase down.

"No, no, your back, husband, I don't want you to hurt your back. Then you will lie groaning in bed for a week!"

"My back feels fine today. It's very strange."

"But a minute ago you complained that you might strain your back."

"Yes, but it feels fine now. Maybe it will hurt later, but let's take advantage of my good health while we can, shall we?"

She pushes, and he pulls the queen-sized bed until it is turned in the opposite direction. Myung Hee can see Yung Chul's scalp through his thinning hair.

Yung Chul straightens up, places one hand on his left hip, and stretches backwards, breathing out a tremendous "Ooof!" as he does so. He walks out the door without kissing Myung Hee goodbye.

After Myung Hee hears his car drive down the street, she runs downstairs. She opens the stereo cabinet in the living room. She inserts a CD and music fills the room.

She circles the room, lifting her faded cotton housedress with her hands as she shuffles her feet, moving her shoulders to the left, to the right, rolling them forward, then backward, just like she saw on MTV. She holds an imaginary microphone to her lips, snapping her fingers up above her head, moving her arms to the left and to the right, then bringing her arms low, first to one side of her hip and then the other.

There was a time when her husband would have joined

her. He used to love to dance. He would hold her in his arms and waltz her across the room, his perfectly round, usually smiling face so serious, watching her with that soft tender look in his eyes, as though he might start crying, a look that made her avert her gaze, humbled and amazed at her power over him. Or he would take her by the hand and twirl her around so her hair would tumble out of its carefully constructed upsweep and the room would spin faster and faster until they both fell, laughing until they cried. Or he might put on an old Chubby Checker record and show her how to twist, his thick black hair combed back until it gleamed, his hands splayed out in front of him as his torso twisted from side to side, his mouth opened in an exaggerated grin so that she had to laugh, he looked so silly!

But now, he complains that she makes too much dust when she dances.

It is when she is dancing that Myung Hee feels the most free. When her feet are moving, her mind has no time to worry, her heart has no time to ache. No energy to feel the shattered dreams, shards of disappointment which every now and then make fresh cuts inside. No desire to cling to hope like a drowning person to a lifesaver, like a newlywed to wedding vows, like an immigrant to the promises of a great land.

Hope — the fairy that was too slow and dimwitted to escape Pandora's box. The one that had sunk its sharp little teeth into Myung Hee's once long and succulent neck and then flown far, far away. But not before sucking all the blood out of her veins, and poisoning her with dreams that had yet to be fulfilled.

Too many dreams unfulfilled breed bitterness. And sometimes, when she compares the way she expected her life to be with the way it is going, it is all Myung Hee can do to keep from dancing out the door.

The paperwork continues to pile up on Yung Chul's desk even as he desperately tries to keep pace with the stream of forms that pours into his In box. He knows that the work will only get worse as the end of the year approaches. The hours will grow longer. His back will ache. His mind will wander. He will start imagining what his life would have been like if . . . if . . .

He picks up a sheet of stationery and runs his fingertips over the engraved letterhead. *Choi & Lee, LLP Certified Public Accountants*. He never intended to be an accountant. He had bigger ideas when he left Korea. This was America. Anything was possible. A poor man could become rich. An unfortunate man could become lucky.

The accounting job was only supposed to be temporary. He needed some way to support his pregnant wife and his baby girl. He would work as an accountant only until they had saved enough money to start their own business, importing celadon pottery perhaps, or opening a chain of Korean restaurants. He would join the legions of other immigrant multimillionaire entrepreneurs who had made the American dream a reality.

But babies cost money, they need to be clothed and fed, and there never seemed to be anything left to save after the groceries were bought and the bills were paid. They were barely making ends meet although he was working fifty, sixty hours a week. But he kept going and going, because if he didn't, who would provide for them? For his darling daughters, his babies who kept him awake at night with their crying, his little girls who ate too much and grew too fast, needing new clothes every other week, and his beautiful wife, his wife who smiled less and less, the love of his life who turned away from him now when he switched off the light, who pretended always to be asleep. He knew she was pretending because she made a light snoring sound, and she never snored when she was really asleep.

Funny how some things changed so little in twenty-five years, while others changed so much. From the outside, his wife looks almost exactly as the day he met her. Yung Chul believes that he can still encircle her waist with both of his hands. He believes this, but he isn't sure since it has been years since he has held his wife that way, dancing with her across the living room floor after their two babies had gone to bed, unable to take his eyes from Myung Hee, or move his hands from her narrow waist, still unable to believe his luck: *This beautiful woman is my wife!* He would have the good fortune of awakening each morning next to this graceful beauty with the moist doe eyes and long movie star lashes. She made him want to sing like Frank Sinatra and dance like Fred Astaire. With a woman like her by his side, his life would be just like the American movies he saw as a youth, movies that always had happy endings.

Yes, to the casual observer Myung Hee looks much the same as she did when she was twenty-one, but Yung Chul knows that she is growing. Her presence now occupies more air, her unhappiness demands more space. The shield around her creates more distance each day, pushing him further and further away. Soon, the barrier surrounding her will take up the entire bed, and he will have to sleep on the sofa in the living room. Her unhappiness will continue to grow. She will fill up their bedroom, and then the upper level of the house, so his children will have to join him on the sofa. They will huddle together for safety and warmth, as the force field around his wife grows, filling up the entire house until finally, the three of them will all have to move away while his wife will stay, occupying every crack and crevice, pushing out the walls with her unfulfilled desires, breaking the windows with her frustrated ambition, hungry for something, always something more.

She wanted a new car, a new refrigerator, a new dishwasher. And when she had those things, she found other things to want. A microwave oven, a cellular phone, a big-screen television. And when he agreed to those, she wanted a bigger car, a colder refrigerator, a quieter dishwasher.

And then one day when his daughters were still in grade school, his wife told him, *told* him, didn't ask him or discuss it with him, but told him that she had decided to give piano lessons to earn some extra money, looking at him with eyes that seemed to say, *Because you are failing us, because you cannot do what you had promised to do when you married me and told me that you loved me oh so many years ago.* Words that she would never say but which she was surely thinking, how could she not? The words were true, weren't they? Yes, they were. He had failed them, failed *her*. He was a failure, as a husband and a father. And a son.

That's when Yung Chul quit listening and started to play more golf. He had spent so many years working more, sleeping less, paying larger bills, yet nothing he did seemed to satisfy his wife. He hadn't meant to give up. He only intended to take a break, try to figure out a better way. There had to be a better way! He couldn't help wondering whether this was what the Fortune Teller meant when she told his mother that he was destined to live his life in unhappiness with the woman he loved so much, but seemed to

12

know less and less each day. Was there anything he could do? Or was it beyond his control, just as his mother had warned?

His wife's arms became large and strong as she lifted the sofa, the table, the television set, rearranging the living room to look bigger, always wanting to improve everything. She began to eat more — consuming raw squid dipped in chili paste, pigs feet pickled in salted vinegar, rice cakes shaped in long cylindrical tubes — and talk less. No longer did she whisper to him words of love and support, or even, as she did later, words of discontent and envy. Now, she fills the air with silence, a constant stream of words unspoken that fills the empty space between them. How he misses her, the woman he married, who he knows is hiding somewhere within the form next to him pretending to be asleep.

Around the time that his younger daughter Grace entered junior high school, he would awaken to find his wife staring at him.

"What are you looking at?" he would ask, in alarm.

"Go to sleep," she replied, staring at him with eyes like saucers.

"I can't sleep when you're staring at me like that."

"Then stay awake with me."

Which, of course, he could not do. He could not bear to watch as she fell out of love, but how to stop it? He had tried everything to keep her, but it was somehow never enough. Never enough! He just wanted to rest, just a few minutes of rest, and he would address his wife's unhappiness later, in the morning, the next day, the next week, the next year, at some time when he had more strength, some time other than now. So he turned away and closed his eyes, and eventually fell asleep, feeling her eyes drilling holes into his back.

About the time that his older daughter Christina entered U.C. Irvine, his wife stopped staring at him. Instead, she sat upright in bed for hours, staring into space, a blank expression on her face. He always pretended to be asleep, feeling as though he had caught her doing something shameful. He knew what she was thinking. She, too, was questioning their ability to fight fate, to forge their own destiny despite the Fortune Teller's predictions.

At about the same time that Myung Hee began to grow, her voice changed. When they first met, it was soft and lilting, as sweet and refreshing as *shikae*. After they moved to the States, it became more like *chige* — comforting, yet still hot and spicy. Now, it is like *kimchee* juice — sour as vinegar with a ripe odor that lingers for hours.

Her discontentment grows every day, follows him to work, lingers in the corners of the house, in his car, reveals itself in every glance, every word, every movement. Her hunger — for what? — makes him want to shrink, make himself as small and inconspicuous as possible. And always, in the back of his mind, he hears his mother's words: *This marriage is doomed. It will not last.*

Chapter 2

"Christina-ya! Grace-ya!"

Myung Hee stands at the foot of the stairs calling her daughters to come and meet their *Chinhominey*. Christina, a second grade teacher at Wilbur Elementary, descends the stairs first, her long glossy hair brushed and neatly pulled back into a pink barrette. She is wearing a peach dress that flows to her ankles and is cinched with a matching belt at her narrow waist. She is 24, the same age as Myung Hee when she left Korea. There is a striking resemblance between mother and daughter. Both women have flawless, translucent complexions, delicate features, and swan-like necks. Myung Hee's face lights up when she sees her daughter, and she avoids looking at her mother-in-law for fear that pride may be interpreted as conceit.

Grace, a senior at U.C.L.A., is shorter, heavier, and two and a half years younger than Christina. Her shoulders slump forward as she follows her sister, tugging at her blue sweat pants and then pulling her hands inside the sleeves of her gray sweatshirt, her hair hanging in her face as though she were a teenage boy instead of an adult woman. Myung Hee sees her mother-in-law's face wrinkle as she scrutinizes her second granddaughter, notices the way her eyes narrow with concern and her shoulders move forward with interest. Myung Hee does not look again at Chinhominey, knowing what she is thinking: *This is the second one. The one with the bad fortune. The reason they left Korea.*

Her daughters drag their feet as they did when they were children, already resentful of this woman who will be staying with them for the next few weeks and for whom they had to devote three whole days to vacuuming, dusting, and mopping the entire house. It is because of her that Grace must sacrifice her bedroom and sleep on the floor in Christina's room.

The woman sitting on the living room couch is old. Her face is puckered like a golden raisin, her gray hair pulled back into a neat bun. Her wire, gold-rimmed glasses give her a severe, schoolmarmish air. She is wearing a brightly colored, traditional Korean dress, with wide sleeves and a fuschia sash tied around her waist. The bow hangs limply by her side. She stares straight ahead as her granddaughters file past and then turns her head to look at them as they stand like tin soldiers, their arms at their sides. She inspects them as though she were looking to buy. The daughters return their grandmother's gaze.

"Greet your Chinhominey," Myung Hee says, visibly embarrassed at her daughters' lack of Korean manners as they stand stiffly, unbowing.

Christina bows awkwardly and smiles.

"*Anyonghasayo,*" she says. Grace does the same when suddenly Chinhominey reaches over and grabs one of Grace's hands. She holds it between her own. She says nothing, peering curiously into her granddaughter's face.

"Did you have a nice flight?" Grace asks in English,

16

glancing uncomfortably at Christina. Chinhominey nods gravely but still doesn't say anything.

"She doesn't speak English," Christina reminds Grace.

"Really no reason to grab me like this," Grace says, a smiling expression masking the meaning of her words. Chinhominey frowns thoughtfully and nods again.

Myung Hee retreats to the kitchen, then brings a steaming pot to the dining room table.

"What's for dinner?" Grace calls out to her mother, extricating herself from Chinhominey's grasp.

Chinhominey says something which makes Myung Hee frown.

"What did she say?" Grace asks.

Myung Hee sets the table, placing the linen napkins next to each plate, then places a pair of silver chopsticks and a spoon on each napkin.

"Your grandmother wants to know why my two grown daughters don't help me prepare dinner," she replies. "You shouldn't ask me what I am making. I should ask you."

"But we never help with dinner," Grace says defensively, her voice rising. "We never even eat dinner at home." Chinhominey looks earnestly at Grace, detecting the anxious tone of her voice.

Her mother stiffens. "Tomorrow, you and Christina will help me make dinner."

Grace turns to Christina, who shrugs her shoulders unsympathetically. Myung Hee calls her husband to dinner.

The Choi family seated around the dining room table, Yung Chul lifts the cover off the casserole. The warm, spicy scent of garlic, peppers, and soy bean paste fills the room.

"Henry won't want to kiss me tonight," Christina whispers to Grace.

Grace ignores her. "Can't we eat something a little more nutritious?" she asks, taking a small sip of the broth. "There's too much salt in this."

"Your grandmother likes chige. Her favorite," Myung Hee replies, nodding in Chinhominey's direction.

Chinhominey makes a noise in the back of her throat and finally she smiles, revealing sharp yellow teeth.

It is a quarter to four the next day, and Grace is trying to leave the house before her mother gets home. Her mother had made it very clear last night that she expected Grace not only to be home for dinner but to *make* dinner. Grace runs down the stairs, hair still wet from a shower, trying to put on a jacket while balancing a pair of high top sneakers and a file folder full of papers in one hand and a backpack in the other. By the time she reaches the bottom of the staircase, her shoes are on her feet, her backpack is on her back, and the papers are scattered all over the living room floor.

"Shit!"

Her mother walks through the front door with a bag full of groceries.

"So messy!" she cries, surveying the scattered papers. She puts the groceries down and wipes her face with the back of her hand. It is almost as hot in September as it was in August.

"I know, I know," Grace says. "I didn't do it on purpose."

She gathers the papers and stuffs them haphazardly into her folder.

"Where are you going?" her mother asks sternly.

"I have an Amnesty meeting to go to."

"No dinner?"

"I can't," Grace says, "I'll help tomorrow. I promise. Bye!"

"Drive careful! Don't forget seatbelt!" her mother calls out.

Her mother is always telling Grace to be careful, drive carefully, watch out, look both ways before crossing — as if Grace were a child! A very stupid child. It is almost as if all her good grades, leadership activities, and community service awards add up to nothing. Her mother still views her as slightly incompetent, a little too clumsy, always comparing her to Christina. And Grace is always falling short, somehow lacking and inadequate, somehow less . . . loveable. Ever since she can remember, it was always, *Why can't you get good grades like Christina?*

And then when she did, when she got *better* grades than her older sister, it was something else.

Why can't you play the piano like Christina?
Why can't you be nice like Christina?
Why can't you be neat like Christina?
Why can't you be pretty like Christina?
Why can't you eat ice cream like Christina?

Grace tried to play the piano, but she had no rhythm. She tried to be neat, hang up her clothes, fix her bed, but the clothes fell off the hangers, the sheets rolled off the bed corners, the ice cream ended up in her nose and in her hair.

Try as she might, she would never be cute and sweet and charming. Not like Christina.

On weekend nights, when she watches her older sister get dressed to go out with her boyfriend, the sweet smell of perfume and apple scented hairspray trailing behind her,

Grace can't help but wonder, *What is wrong with me? Why doesn't anyone want me?*

Myung Hee stands by the front door, listening, and waiting. Waiting to hear the awful screeching sound of brakes as Grace's car crashes into a truck, or a lamp post. She waits, listening as the car starts up and then drives down the street. Only then does she allow herself to breathe.

It could happen at anytime. And then her second daughter that she loves, that she scolds and criticizes too much, would be taken from her.

It is hard to keep her distance, but she must, she has told herself. It is difficult to hold back, but more difficult to love someone when you know that you will suffer for it. Harder to love someone when you know that she will be taken from you, suddenly, without warning, without even a chance to say goodbye.

She tries to put away thoughts about Grace, but her movements are slow, her mind distracted. *Why is Chinhominey visiting, now, after all these years?* Of course, it is her right, as the mother of Yung Chul, as the grandmother of Grace and Christina. It is only natural for a grandmother to want to see her granddaughters, but she wonders whether there is another reason for Chinhominey's visit. Why *now*, after all this time? She wrings her hands anxiously, staring out the kitchen window, for it has become part of Myung Hee's nature to worry. After all, she is, above all else, a mother. A mother who can't help but love her children. It's not the same for a father, she knows. A father can love his children without getting too close, without hurting himself, without giving too much of himself away, just like he can love a woman, without pain, without losing himself.

A man's love is limited by who he is and what he is willing to give. It is not the bittersweet love of a woman that overwhelms, frightens, tries to control, remains uncontrollable.

A woman becomes her children, just as they were once a part of her. A child receives life inside her mother, physically becoming a part of her, before being wrenched away, taking a piece of her, leaving a space, leaving her less than she was. Longing for something to fill the emptiness, take away the loneliness. Knowing that possession will never be had the way it once was when two were literally one.

The irony of childbirth, the cruelty of having to fight for what will be lost, having to fight in order that it may be lost.

With Grace, the cruelty was compounded. She would be twice lost, once in childbirth, again in death.

A child should never die before her mother. It is against nature.

Her first child entered the world easily, the way first born children usually do not. It was different the second time. Myung Hee gave birth to Grace over a period of several days and nights. Pain and happiness and boredom (yes, even boredom!) and expectation and dread, so many emotions filling her up, then tearing her apart.

The contractions came slowly at first, but so deep, she could feel them pressing against her insides. The baby refused to come out, stubbornly clinging to her mother, who was perhaps unwilling to let go, unwilling to push out her child, thrust her into a world that would consume her.

The contractions came faster, so fast that Myung Hee couldn't breathe, until she felt she would die, and then she didn't have to force herself anymore, she didn't even have to try. She wanted to keep her baby, keep it safe inside, but it was too late, too late, and then a feeling of tremendous relief, of joy, sweet joy, my baby! And the sound of the baby crying, and the feel of Myung Hee's own tears, rolling down her cheeks and into her open mouth, for she was also crying, tears of joy, of sorrow, of relief, arms outstretched, longing to feel, to touch, to hold. Where are they taking my baby? Why are they taking her away? And then Myung Hee felt it, the space, the tiny space where the baby had been.

Chapter 3

Chinhominey is sitting on the new patterned twill couch in the Choi's living room, hands on knees, like royalty waiting to be served. National Geographic magazines fan out in a large wicker basket underneath the glass coffee table. A row of celadon bowls are lined upon a shelf in the display case, each bowl on the right slightly larger than its neighbor to the left. Pictures of the Choi family cover the end table next to the couch. One picture captures Christina in her graduation robe, clutching a diploma in her hand. She is smiling with her mouth closed, her eyes serious. Another picture frames the entire family at an amusement park when the girls are much younger. Grace's hair sticks up like cotton candy. She is laughing, candied apple in hand, red glaze smeared around her mouth. Christina is standing near Grace, her hands folded neatly in front of her. She is smiling with the same closed mouth expression that Chinhominey noticed in the graduation picture.

Chinhominey shakes her head slowly, frown lines dragging down both sides of her own mouth. She glances around the room, which appears well-kept and orderly. But

Chinhominey notices that the dates on the magazines are several years old. The bowls on the display shelf need to be dusted; she can see the thick layer of dust even from where she sits across the room. But the pictures cause her the most concern. Among these family pictures, there is not one photograph of herself.

Myung Hee carries a large silver breakfast tray containing a bowl of assorted fruit slices, toast, and coffee. Chinhominey stares apprehensively at the tray as Myung Hee in her faded blue housedress makes her way across the room. Myung Hee tightens her grip and continues walking. She carefully sets the tray down on the table.

"I expected you to drop it," Chinhominey says. She is using the familiar Korean, the grammatical form used to address intimates, or children, or those who are inferior in social status.

Myung Hee smiles politely.

"But as usual, you disappointed my expectations," Chinhominey adds. Myung Hee's smile disappears.

"Maybe you could have better expectations," Myung Hee suggests, although she knows that she should bite her tongue.

"You are still stubborn as always," Chinhominey says, "Unable to take criticism."

She takes a sip of coffee and adds more wrinkles to her face.

"Tastes terrible," she complains, pointing to her cup. "Needs more sugar."

Myung Hee dumps a teaspoonful of sugar into her mother-in-law's proffered cup and smiles with gritted teeth. Chinhominey takes another sip of coffee, pauses, as though trying to discern any bitterness in her drink, and says nothing. Myung Hee accepts her silence as a compliment and sits beside her.

The women do not look at each other. The only sound is the slurping noise Chinhominey makes as she drinks her coffee.

"How are you and your husband?" Chinhominey finally asks.

"Fine, fine. Never better," Myung Hee says firmly. Her chin is tilted slightly upward as she looks her mother-in-law directly in the eyes.

"Better than what? Better than nothing is still nothing."

"We have a very good marriage. Very happy," Myung Hee declares, straining to keep the irritation out of her voice.

Chinhominey sniffs contemptuously and takes another sip of coffee.

"What about your children?"

"Fine, fine. You saw how they are," Myung Hee says, using a smile to dilute the defensiveness of her tone.

"I wouldn't have recognized them. They have no manners. They are like Americans."

"They *are* Americans," Myung Hee says firmly.

"They still have Korean faces. They will always have Korean faces."

"Those are American faces, too," Myung Hee says, struggling to keep her expression pleasant. Her left eye twitches with the effort.

Chinhominey sniffs again, "It is because of you that they have such bad attitudes. They only think about themselves. You wait. When you are old and alone, they won't take care of you. They'll give you to a hospital. American people don't take care of their parents. There's no place for old people in this country."

"I am very proud of my children. Unlike American girls, Christina has come home to live until she marries. Today, even girls in Korea do not behave so obediently. You see, she is not so selfish."

"And the second? The one who does not dress like a girl?"

Myung Hee shifts in her seat and takes a long sip before answering. She returns the cup to the saucer, hand shaking slightly so coffee splashes onto the table. Myung Hee makes no effort to wipe it up.

"The second is studying in college and gets only the highest marks. She will go to law school next year." Her voice is steady but her hands still tremble.

Chinhominey leans over and stabs a piece of strawberry with a fork. She pops it into her mouth and chews thoughtfully.

"She is the one who will bring you heartbreak."

"Nonsense!" Myung Hee's voice rises.

"The one who will die young."

"Superstition!" Myung Hee cries, clapping her hands over her ears.

"You never listen," Chinhominey says, red juice leaking out of the corners of her mouth.

"Why should I listen? Listen to what? Old wives' tales! Old Korean superstitions!"

"You mock destiny and you will be the first to regret it!"

Myung Hee visibly contains her anger by breathing

deeply through her nose, closing her eyes briefly and then exhaling.

"Would you like more coffee?" Myung Hee asks, turning her head in Chinhominey's direction but avoiding the other woman's unyielding gaze.

"Your family is falling apart. Like she predicted."

"Toast?" Myung Hee asks, rising from the couch.

"You never listen. I can see your marriage is no good. You and your husband never look at each other when you speak. Your children don't like each other. You refuse to see the signs. The Fortune Teller warned you. You cannot change fate."

Chinhominey takes a sip of coffee and her expression changes.

"Blech! Ayyyewww!!" she cries, making a flicking motion with her tongue, "Blech!! Ayy!! You put poison in my coffee!"

Yung Chul runs downstairs, his hands pressed against the sides of his head. *What is all that yelling?* He looks at his mother, searching for an explanation.

"She tried to kill me!"

Yung Chul raises his eyebrows and turns to his wife. Myung Hee looks back at her husband, her eyes round with confusion.

"Why would I want to kill her? So she may die on my new couch?"

Chinhominey starts wailing again. Christina and Grace, hearing the commotion, hurry into the room.

"What's all the racket?" Grace asks.

"Your grandmother is having a temper tantrum," Myung Hee replies.

Chinhominey stops wailing and glares at Myung Hee.

27

The two women stare at each other with round accusatory eyes and pinched angry mouths stained strawberry red. Their heads are pulled back on their necks like circling gamecocks.

Christina purses her mouth and wrings her hands as she tries to think of a way to tactfully mediate. Grace, her arms folded across her chest, one hip thrust forward, rolls her eyes and glares at Chinhominey. She had a feeling that this woman would be bad news!

"Your grandmother ate fruit and drank coffee at the same time so her tongue feels prickly. She has no common sense," Myung Hee says. "If she did, she would know that I would never poison her in my own house. It's bad luck to have someone die in your house."

"I thought you didn't believe in old wives' tales," Chinhominey says. She makes more flicking motions with her tongue, as though she were trying to rid her mouth of cat hair. "What a disappointment," she says quietly, "What a disappointment to have a son who prefers his wife over his own mother."

She stands up. Her posture is sadly slumped, defeated. She shuffles away.

"Your mother is an actress," Myung Hee says, leaning over the coffee table to gather the coffee cups and forks. "A bad actress."

Yung Chul gives her a sharp look. "She is getting old. We have not seen her in a long time."

His voice is harsher than he had intended. Myung Hee glares at him, her mouth curved downward with indignation. "Age is not excuse for everything. She has always been this way. So unreasonable! So unfair to me!"

"Why do you have to be so stubborn?" Yung Chul's voice has lost its edge. His arms hang limply by his sides.

"I'm not stubborn. You always side with your mother." Myung Hee turns away from her husband, her arms folded across her chest. Yung Chul takes a couple of steps toward her.

"If that were true, I would not be standing here with you. We would not be here in the United States. We would not have our two children."

Grace and Christina look at each other puzzled, *They must have misunderstood?* Their father opens his mouth to say more, but conscious of his daughters' presence, changes his mind and marches upstairs. Myung Hee storms into the kitchen and begins to scrub the tile floor. She always cleans the house when she's upset.

"What was all that about?" Grace asks, bursting with curiosity, "Why did Chinhominey scream at you?"

"Chinhominey believes in superstition and jinxes," Myung Hee says, starting to get angry all over again. "That is all she can talk about. Only ghost stories."

"She means spirits," Christina says. She understands a few more Korean words than Grace.

Myung Hee straightens up, twisting her neck first to the left and then to the right. The tension being released makes a loud popping sound. She says, "Chinhominey is superstitious. Old stories. You don't need to know."

"Know what?"

"Know what the Fortune Teller said. Anyway, it doesn't matter. Lies. She is an old lady telling lies."

"Lies about what?"

29

"Ayyy!" Myung Hee says, shaking her head. "If you have nothing to do, help me scrub the floor."

"I've got to get ready for work," Christina says. "My kids will be waiting. I'll be home around five."

"I have to run, too. I have class in less than half an hour," Grace says, "I'll be home around six."

"I thought so," Myung Hee sighs, as her daughters leave the kitchen. "Too busy to help your mother but not too busy to ask stupid questions." She rearranges her housedress, sits back on her heels, and pushes away loose strands of hair with the back of her hand. She picks up the rag and starts to wipe again at the shiny linoleum floor. She listens for the sound of her husband's footsteps on the stairs, imagines him walking into the kitchen, looking for her now that the children have left the room.

The man she married would never have tolerated an unresolved argument. The man she married would have come into the room and apologized, not because he was wrong and she was right, but because she was upset and he was sorry. And she would have accepted his apology and proffered one of her own, not because she felt obliged, but because he cared. When they were all living under the same roof in Korea, he *could* defend her to his mother. He would always side with his wife then. Even when she suggested that they move out of his family home, the place where he was born and where he grew up, he did not protest.

It will be impossible to create a happy life together when every day we hear from your mother how our marriage is doomed, she had told him, clasping her hands together, her long slender fingers anxiously intertwined. *Let's go to America where we can create our own destiny.*

She had read an article in a magazine about a young

30

Korean couple, just like them but poor and uneducated, who went to America and made a fortune selling celadon vases. *If they can do it, we can,* she told him, *We can open a gift shop or a restaurant.* It didn't really matter *what* they did, what mattered was that they would create their future *together,* discuss matters — customers, inventory, employees — practical matters that would bring them closer together as they pursued their shared entrepreneurial dream.

He had nodded, swept away by his young wife's radiance, her hopefulness, agreeing so readily that she believed it was a mutual decision. They would move to America. They would start over. They would never again discuss Chinhominey's dire predictions. And because their memory of Chinhominey had become inextricably linked to her words of doom, they would only rarely mention her name.

But an only child cannot forget his mother so easily, Myung Hee learned. Even though Yung Chul did not speak of his mother, he thought of her often. She began to feel a nagging guilt that perhaps *she* was responsible for having coaxed her husband into leaving his mother behind.

Myung Hee sensed her husband's torn loyalties, sensed his own guilt. One morning, when the girls were still too young to be in school, Myung Hee walked outside to place some bills in the mailbox at the curb. She was surprised to see her husband's car was still in the driveway, even though he had kissed her goodbye a half-hour earlier. Had he taken the bus to work? She walked cautiously toward the parked car, her forehead wrinkled with worry, her heart pounding. She peered into the window and saw her husband, her beloved husband, sitting in the driver's seat, dressed in his navy blue business suit, his hands wrapped around the steering wheel, his eyes staring straight ahead. Although it was nearly eighty degrees, the windows were rolled up. He was crying, tears streaming down his cheeks, not bothering to wipe them away. His gaze was elsewhere, past the windshield, beyond the house where he lived with his two daughters and his wife. The tears fell, one by one, sliding down his cheeks, dropping off his chin, splashing onto his suit, his silk tie.

Something made her turn and walk away then, something told her that she must not let him know that she had seen him. She crept into the house and sat on the couch, stunned. Had he lost his job? What could make him behave this way? Then she remembered: *Today was Chinhominey's birthday.*

She tilted her head, at first unable to digest this realization. She wondered what it meant, what it could mean, when a husband can no longer share his feelings with his wife.

She cried herself then, for her lonely husband, for the future of her family. For guilt had created a space between them where before there was none.

Chapter 4

While his wife is fending off his daughter's questions, Yung Chul stands outside Grace's bedroom door, trying to decide whether to knock. His mother makes the decision by scolding him through the closed door, "What are you doing? Spying on your own mother?"

He opens the door. His mother is sitting on the edge of the bed glaring at him.

"I was not spying," he says. "*Uhmahnee*, why have you become so sensitive in your old age?"

"What do you call it," she says, "if not spying when you stand outside the door like a prison guard without saying anything?"

"I was trying to decide whether you were taking a nap," he says.

"How could I take a nap after having argued with your wife?"

"I was only thinking of your feelings, Uhmahnee," he says, trying hard to control his voice.

He stands awkwardly by the door. It has been a long time since he has interacted with his mother, and he has forgotten how to behave. The feelings of uncertainty, however, return as familiar as ever. He is reduced to the status of a child, an only son, awaiting his mother's harsh judgment.

"If you had thought of my feelings, you would not have disobeyed me so many years ago. Or is it easier to forget your filial loyalty when you are an American? I do not ask much of you. I do not expect you to behave like a Korean anymore. I do not expect you to provide me with a home and to take care of me in my old age."

Yung Chul closes his eyes. Swallowed pride and percolating anger were easier to digest than raw guilt. He had hoped, foolishly, that his mother would have forgiven him. He had not intended to desert her. He merely wanted to have the freedom to live his own life.

You chose to pursue your own happiness instead of fulfilling your obligation to your mother.

She was right. He had been selfish. But did he regret? He feels the blood drain from his face.

"I am sleepy now," she says, "I would like to take a nap."

He walks slowly out of the room, shutting the door behind him. Doubt — for so long a visitor in his head — has now entered his heart.

He is walking to the car when he hears a buzzing by his ear. He turns his head. It is a dragonfly.

Funny, he thinks, he has not seen a dragonfly in a long time.

A very long time.

"Amma, what is that?"

He was just a little boy, maybe six or seven.

34

"It's a dragonfly," his mother said, looking up at the sky.

"What does a dragonfly do?"

"Many things," she said.

"What kinds of things?"

She smiled. Her lips were painted red as though she were going to a party. She was proud of her good looks, her thick dark eyebrows, her pale complexion. She always looked as though she were expecting important guests even though they rarely had visitors. She dressed in colorful silks imported from China and sewn into dresses in Japan. She was as bright as the sun to her only child.

"Wait here," she said, "just a few minutes."

She hurried into the house, moving quickly in her long orange skirt. When she returned, she was carrying a long piece of string and a paper bag.

"Where is the dragonfly?" she asked.

Yung Chul pointed to a nearby puddle.

His mother stepped into the puddle with her shiny red high heels, causing ripples on the water's surface. The dragonfly flew away from the water. His mother leapt up, waving the paper bag into the air, and caught the dragonfly!

"Amma! Amma! Let me look!" Yung Chul cried.

His mother reached into the paper bag and pulled out her fist.

"Where's the dragonfly?" the boy asked, taking the paper bag from his mother and looking inside.

His mother cupped one hand over the other.

"Look," she said, creating a small space between her hands. He peered into the space and saw the dragonfly fluttering its wings, making a buzzing noise.

"Does it hurt?" he asked. "Does it hurt your hand?"

"No."

"Does it hurt the dragonfly?"

"Some creatures can't feel pain," she replied.

"What are you going to do with it?" he asked.

His mother curled one hand around the dragonfly, but not so tightly that it would be crushed. With her other hand, she reached into the front pocket of her orange skirt and pulled out the long piece of string. She poked the string through a hole in the tip of the dragonfly's abdomen, as though she were threading the eye of a needle.

"Are you taking it prisoner?" he asked.

"No," she said. She opened her hand so that the dragonfly flew away, but continued to hold onto the string with her other hand. As the dragonfly flew higher and higher into the sky, she released more string. She started to run, the dragonfly flying above her like a kite in the sky. Yung Chul chased after his mother, shouting, "Let me try! Let me try!"

His mother stopped running and handed him the end of the string. He held onto it, watching the dragonfly buzz overhead.

"What do I do?" he cried.

"Run!" his mother replied, "But be careful. Don't pull on the string too tightly or you will hurt it. Don't run too fast or too slow. You must be the same speed as the dragonfly or you will kill it."

So he ran, the dragonfly flying above him. He felt a powerful bond between the insect and himself, connected only by a string to the other so high in the sky, sailing in the wind. He watched, fascinated by his living kite, and ran faster and faster, watching as the dragonfly floated in the clouds, such a beautiful sight!

So fascinated was Yung Chul, his head turned toward the heavens, that he did not see the rock that he tripped upon, that made him fall onto the hard, wet grass, pulling the string down suddenly with him.

His mother ran over to where the boy lay in the grass. "Are you okay?" she asked.

The boy stood up.

"Where's the dragonfly?" he asked, looking around, searching the area nearby, "Where's the string?"

Yung Chul found the string in the grass. He followed the string to the end and found the dragonfly, its wings no longer fluttering. There was no buzzing noise, no longer the sound of anything but the wind.

His mother placed one hand on his shoulder as the little boy wept.

"You should have paid attention to where you were going," she said.

The little boy sobbed even harder. So sorry was he for the dragonfly! "I didn't see the rock!" he cried, "I didn't see it! It wasn't my fault!"

His mother gently scolded him, "Of course it was your fault. You were the only one holding the string."

Chapter 5

The only thing I ever wanted was a happy family. But it was the one thing that was denied me. To my daughter-in-law, I am a witch. To my son, I am a heavy burden. To my granddaughters, I am a stranger. In the eyes of my family, I am uglified, disfigured with the truth, hideous with expectation. But in reality, I am not bad looking for a sixty-four-year-old. I don't deny it, I don't pretend to be modest in the disingenuous way of many women. I look good for my age. I have a mirror. I know it. My eyes are bright, my eyebrows still dark. My posture is straight, my back uncurved. My hands are still long and graceful. But being good looking for a sixty-four-year-old is not the same as being good looking for a twenty-four-year-old. Or even a forty-four-year-old. And it's not the same as being good looking. My eyes still sparkle the way they used to, but my eyelashes have fallen out. Around my mouth, lines have deepened, dragging my lips down into a perpetual frown. The skin across my forehead and cheeks is rough and mottled with age spots. I am fortunate that I have my front teeth, even though several of my back ones have fallen out. My once thick black hair is now sparse and gray.

Once, I had it all, looks, intelligence, love. I was fortunate enough to have a husband provide me with land as well as love. I was smart enough to hold onto that land until its value had increased twentyfold. Four decades ago, I had everything: I had an obedient son; I had a husband who loved me more than he loved his work. He brought me gifts from faraway places — China, Hong Kong, Japan. He gave me love, devotion and security and what did I give him in return? Lies, deceit, worry, fear. But also love. For I did love my husband, but what do you know when you are only seventeen years old? You don't even know how little you know. You think you know all the answers. Even worse, you think you know the questions.

In my case, I didn't know either. I can admit that now even though I don't know what good it does. Like many tragedies, my mistake was the result of good intentions. I blame my husband's mother. A fat-bellied woman lacking humor. She came into my room every morning, after her son had left for work.

"A son," she demanded, her breath as sour and unpleasant as her bloated face, "Where is my grandson?"

So I started to search. I searched in my bed, the bed I shared with my husband. I searched my head, hoping that if I focused all my energies on creating a son, my body would obey. I even searched my heart, wondering whether I was withholding this gift to my husband in order to punish his nagging mother. But it wasn't until I searched the twisted mind of fate that I found him. The son I was never supposed to have.

I had heard about the Fortune Teller even before I met her. She had no name. Everyone referred to her simply as the Fortune Teller. Everyone knew she had extraordinary powers. Her existence was whispered about among my parents' friends when I was a girl. Some believed she was a sorceress. Others, including my parents, believed that she was a type of mad scientist whose predictions were an accurate interpretation of the way things were meant to be.

She lived in a wooden shack partially obscured by maple trees several miles outside our village. If you didn't already know where the old woman lived, you wouldn't find out by accident. I had followed my own mother there several times as a young girl. I tried to ring the doorbell, but I couldn't find one. I was about to knock on the wooden door, when it opened.

The Fortune Teller looked about ninety-nine years old. Her face was gnarled, resembling a dried shitake mushroom before it is soaked in water. So many wrinkles! Her back was stooped, her shoulders hunched forward. But her heavy-lidded eyes were lively as a child's, darting about, so curious! Inside, her house was cold and dark. Sheets of brown paper covered the windows.

"Sit down," she said. I sat down on a small chair with silk lining. The silk was cool against my legs and made me shiver.

The Fortune Teller poured us both a cup of tea. "I have questions about the future," I told her.

She nodded, opened her mouth as if to speak, and belched instead. She took another sip of tea and belched again. Then she asked for my birth information. I told her where, when, and how I was born. Did I come out head first? Was it a doctor or a midwife who first laid hands on me? Was my father present? She told me the alignment of the stars at the time of my birth and nodded her head without telling me why she did so. I told her about my husband.

I told her that he was a kind man with a good heart. I told her that we were very happy, our life together was perfect. Except for one thing.

"His mother?" she guessed.

"Two things," I corrected myself.

"You want a son," she said.

"Yes."

She nodded. It was a story she had heard before. She got up from her chair and walked with unsteady steps into the only other room in the house. She returned carrying a large black book in her hands.

She asked me for my husband's age and the date and time of his birth. Then she consulted the big black book. She frowned and shook her head. She turned the page, frowned, and shook her head again.

"What's the matter?"

"You will not have a son with this man," the old woman said.

"What?"

"You will not have any children with this man."

She shut the book and looked up at me. She took another long swallow of tea. She poured us both some more tea although my cup was still nearly full.

"You must have made a mistake," I said, "Perhaps I gave you the wrong time. Perhaps I was born at 1:32 in the morning and not in the afternoon."

The old woman examined me with her furrowed face, her eyes piercing underneath heavy eyelids.

"It is not you. It is your husband. He is not destined to have children. He is the end of the line."

I knew that neither my husband nor my mother-in-law would be pleased with that news. In fact, the news might so displease them that they might arrange for my husband to take a mistress. They might even throw me out of the house! The blood rushed to my cheeks, my forehead glistened with perspiration. I looked at the Fortune Teller pleadingly, trying to keep the tears from spilling out of my eyes. "What can I do?" I asked. I was only seventeen years old. Too young to have my life end.

Fortunately, the old woman had not only the power to look into the future but, like God, she had the power to change it.

"You must have a son," she replied.

"But you told me that I couldn't have any children."

"You do not listen carefully," she said, "I said your husband could never have a son. You can have as many children as you like."

"I don't understand," I said. You see how naive I was at that age?

"Your husband is not the only man capable of fathering a child."

I stared at the old woman in disbelief.

"That is not an appropriate thing to joke about," I replied in as stern a tone as a seventeen-year-old can conjure. And you know what she did? The old woman laughed! She laughed at me, making such a gurgling sound I thought she was choking.

"Did I say something funny?" I asked. My face was red with embarrassment and confusion.

"I only give advice," she said, "I cannot force you to take it."

She closed the big black book in front of her and folded her hands on top of it. Then she closed her eyes and fell asleep.

The next morning, after my husband had left for work, my mother-in-law again knocked on my door.

"Where is my grandson?" she asked.

"Why," I answered, "did you run out of things to eat?"

She looked at me for a moment with a puzzled expression, as though she didn't understand what I had said.

"What?" she asked.

"I think I will go for a walk today," I told her.

I blame my mother-in-law for what happened next. If she had not pestered me, things might have turned out differently. I blame her, but I do not regret. For I love my son, even though I was tricked into having him. Even though, he is a reminder of how I naively betrayed my husband.

Chapter 6

Christina stands in the middle of the kitchen, the sharp scent of sautéed garlic and the warm aroma of seaweed soup filling the air. Her mother stands behind her by the sink, unsheathing cloves of garlic. Grace stir-fries spinach. Christina is admiring the ring that Henry gave to her the night before. It's not an engagement ring, she explains, but a friendship ring. Her mother peers over Christina's shoulder. "What is friendship ring for?" she asks.

"To show me that he's serious," she says. The fluorescent light in the kitchen bounces off the ring's many facets.

"Excuse me," Grace says, pushing past her sister to return the sesame oil to the cabinet. The kitchen is large enough that Grace could walk around Christina without touching her, but she bumps into Christina again on the way back to the stove. Grace has had enough of Christina's mooning over Henry. Grace has had enough of Christina, *period*. Chinhominey is staying in Grace's bedroom, and Grace has been sleeping on the floor in Christina's room for almost a week now. The floral prints decorating Christina's bedroom walls are closing in on her, and the lace-covered boudoir pillows placed at jaunty angles on her bed annoy her with their banality. She is tired of waking to the *psssssttt* sound of aerosol hairspray and the suffocating smell of toxins being released into the air. But what she hates the most is having to listen to Christina coo and sigh to her dorky boyfriend every night for an hour or more. The only thing she hates more than Christina's soft, high-pitched, lovey-dovey voice is Christina's condescending, pitying, big sister voice as she asks Grace about her nonexistent boyfriends. Grace bangs the wooden spoon against the Teflon pan as she pushes the spinach leaves around. She turns to get a plate from the cabinet.

Christina steps out of Grace's way and holds four fingers out in front of her. Her lips are pressed together in a dreamy smile, her head tilted to one side as she admires her present. She is swaying as she stands, moving slightly from side to side as though slowdancing with an invisible partner.

"It's an emerald," she says proudly. "He knows that I love the color green."

"Good for you," Myung Hee says. She starts to chop smooth cloves of garlic with a butcher knife. "He makes good husband."

"Why? Just because he buys her jewelry?" Grace asks as she pulls a dinner plate out of the cupboard.

Christina looks at her, putting one hand on her hip, and rolls her eyes. "Somebody's jealous," she says. "I don't see guys lining up to buy you jewelry."

"Maybe because I don't advertise myself for sale," Grace says, using the wooden spoon to push the spinach leaves out of the pan and onto the plate.

"No more fighting. What's the matter with you? You

should love each other," Myung Hee scolds. She stops chopping and looks sharply at Grace.

"The way she's dressed, who could love her?" Christina says, pointing her chin at her sister. Grace's blue sweatshirt is torn at the cuffs and clashes with her green army pants.

Christina raises her hand again, so that the light reflects off the emerald.

"It's good quality," her mother says, looking over Christina's shoulder and observing the ring.

"And it's big," Christina adds.

"Why does everyone in this family have to be so materialistic?" Grace asks, dumping some chopped green onions into the frying pan. She doesn't see the point of spending money on something that serves no useful purpose. If *she* had a ring like that, she would probably lose it anyway, she tells herself. It would slip off her finger and down the drain when she washed her hands, or she would leave it at the gym and somebody would steal it.

"It's not to fight that I ask you to come downstairs and help with dinner," Myung Hee says.

Her mother's rebuke seems to be directed at Grace, not Christina. *It's not fair,* Grace thinks. Chinhominey walks into the kitchen.

"Grandmother's here," Myung Hee warns in English. Then, to her mother-in-law, she asks in Korean, "Did you have a nice nap?"

Christina opens the cabinet and takes out the dinner plates. Grace opens a drawer and takes out five spoons and five pairs of lacquered wood chopsticks. Chinhominey sits at the table, peering over the top of her glasses at each of her granddaughters in turn and then at Myung Hee. "Why do my grandchildren always fight?" Chinhominey asks.

46

"Did their arguing wake you?"

"I cannot understand why they like to argue so much."

Grace and Christina roll their eyes at each other. They know enough Korean to understand that their grandmother is complaining about them. Again.

"But what can I expect? It's not their fault. It's fate," Chinhominey says, "they can't fight fate."

"Ayyy! Enough talk about your silly superstition," Myung Hee says. She continues mincing garlic. Grace watches her for a minute, fascinated yet frightened. Her mother chops rapidly, and the large butcher knife comes dangerously close to her fingers. Grace has seen her mother mince garlic enough times to know that she won't cut herself, but each time the possibility dances in front of Grace, transfixes her. What would happen if her mother were careless, inattentive?

Whack!

Grace shudders, closing her eyes as she visualizes fingertips crawling across the countertop.

How long have you had this problem?

Bad thoughts, evil thoughts, unpleasant thoughts. Unshakable thoughts. A nasty little voice whispering in Grace's ear, crawling in her mind, insinuating itself in her brain, Imagine this! *What if?* The more horrible the thought, the more difficult it is to erase it from her mind, banish it from her consciousness. Trying not to think about it makes her think about it, the act of negation an act of affirmation, the act of trying to forget being the very thing that forces her to remember. The horrible images protect her, divert her thoughts away from Christina and her emerald ring, her perfect skin, her straight white teeth.

"What's the matter with your daughter?" Chinhominey

47

asks, her brow furrowed anxiously. "Why does she have a sour face?"

Myung Hee looks at her younger daughter and shakes her head. Grace's eyes are tightly closed, her lips pursed together, her shoulders hunched toward her neck.

Chapter 7

The Coalition For Reproductive Freedom meets the second Monday of every month unless there's an emergency, such as an abortion clinic protest, the reason for tonight's special meeting. At six o'clock, Grace has to be at a For the Sake of Children meeting on the other side of town, and at seven-thirty, she has an Organization to Stop Hunger meeting on campus.

Grace stops at a red light and runs her fingers through her damp hair. She glances in the rearview mirror. Her hair is matted down to her forehead. After the meeting, she is going to meet some friends from her American History class for coffee. She has a crush on one of them. She fluffs her hair, to no avail. She still looks like one of the Beatles, the dark fringe of hair skimming the bridge of her nose. Oh well, she tells herself, it just looks weird because you are adhering to traditional notions of beauty — a thought that reminds her to go to the Feminist Undergrad Society reception on Thursday night. They will be electing officers and although Grace knows that she shouldn't — her schedule is hectic enough as it is — her friend Marlene wants her to volunteer for President. It's not a competitive election and often there are several co-Presidents — the women's alternative to male power politics.

She glances at her watch as she pulls into the YWCA parking lot. Late as usual, but only by fifteen minutes.

If Grace had known that the Grinder was a sports bar rather than a coffeehouse, she would have suggested another place for their rendezvous. She spots Mike, Castor, and Jerry seated at a booth in the corner. Mike looks up and waves her over.

"Sorry I'm late," she says, breathlessly, "I had a meeting."

"Busy as usual," Mike says, flashing his teeth at her. "You're the busiest person I know. And the smartest."

Grace looks down, embarrassed. She orders a cappuccino from a waitress who is dressed in a cheerleader's uniform.

"What? You don't drink?" Mike asks, giving her a nudge with his elbow. His perpetual tan has a fresh glow. He must have been riding his bike this afternoon.

"I have to drive home," she says, although the truth is that she doesn't want to participate in this frat-boy sports bar scene. Her nonalcoholic beverage is her way to silently protest this sexist watering hole. She catches Mike's eyes roam over the waitress' legs.

"Who picked this place anyway?" she asks.

"We always come here."

"Really?" she asks, "Why?"

Mike points at the big screen television. A large beefy man wearing a helmet and a uniform is dancing around with a football.

The waitress brings her cappuccino. The crowd of men

standing in front of the television shout "Yes!" and hi-five each other.

"Touchdown," Mike says.

Grace takes a sip of her coffee. Everybody yells "Dude!" and slaps hi-fives again.

"Another touchdown?"

"No, a Nike ad," Castor replies.

Mike turns to her, smiling again. Grace tells herself that he is too blonde, his eyes too blue. He is too shallow, too much the stereotype of the All-American frat boy, an icon of collegiate chauvinism, a symbol of everything she disdains. Still, every time he smiles at her, her stomach does backflips.

"What are you doing Friday night?" he asks.

"Nothing," she lies. She has to volunteer at the battered women's shelter.

"Great," he says, his sapphire orbs gleaming. "You want to get together?"

She nods her head, not trusting herself with words, thinking to herself, *A date! With Mike Johnson!*

She picks up her coffee cup and accidentally brushes Mike's tanned forearm. She can't help but notice the veins on the back of his hand, running along his wrist. She takes a sip of coffee and swallows hard.

"Is that a yes or a no?"

"Sure," she says, trying to sound calm.

"Great. That midterm's going to be a real bitch."

"Yeah," Grace says. It is the fall semester of her senior year, and she isn't too concerned about her grade point average. By the time grades were posted, she would have already submitted her law school applications.

"We were thinking about meeting at Elizabeth's place."

51

"Elizabeth?" Grace asks, "Who's Elizabeth?"

"My girlfriend," Mike says, scribbling an address on a cocktail napkin.

Grace, her eyes downcast, feels as though someone has just pushed her off a boat into icy waters. She swallows the last of her cappuccino. The bitter aftertaste lingers in her mouth.

"I'll see you guys later," she says, standing up to leave.

Mike gives her a brief smile and then turns back to the game.

This time, his smile gives her a stomach ache.

A little after ten o'clock, she walks into the kitchen and picks up the receiver to call Marcie, to remind her about the Amnesty International meeting. Christina is already on the phone.

"It's only been an hour since we saw each other."

"I know, but I can't help it," Henry says, his voice whiny and pathetic, "I really miss you."

It reminds Grace of high school. The phone rang for Christina all the time then, too. While the boys in Grace's class tortured her by calling her names like "Chink" and "Nip," the boys in Christina's class wrote her love notes and left candy bars in her locker. Race didn't seem to matter for beautiful women.

Grace had consoled herself by thinking that when she turned sixteen, her skin would clear up, her chest would fill out, and her hair would finally lie flat. Five years later, her face still broke out, she was still a 32A, and her hair still did exactly the opposite of what she wanted it to do. No matter how many aerobics classes she sweated through, her legs were not long and slender like Christina's but thick and shapeless, *daikon dahty.* Her mother often claimed that Grace took after her father's side of the family, a statement that Grace accepted as a form of disownment. It didn't help that when her mother lamented Grace's freckled face, her Korean accent made it sound as though she were calling her daughter's visage "fucker face."

Chapter 8

Yung Chul opens his eyes in the darkness, but lies very, very still. He feels his wife's presence in the bed next to him, knows that she is awake without even looking. He can almost hear the wheels in her head. He can feel her frustration rise like steam from her body. For the hundredth, no, thousandth, time he asks himself,

When did his wife become so . . . unhappy? When did they stop talking? When did his marriage become so joy- less?

A silent truce is all they have left. He doesn't even know what Myung Hee thinks about. There was a time when he could tell, by the look in her eyes, the tone of her voice, the way she held her hands, waving them around excitedly or wringing them in her lap when she was nervous.

She was a freshman at Seoul University and he a senior when they first met. She was even more charming than she was pretty, always surrounded by a group of friends, the center of attention. She had some admirers, awkward young men who followed her around, left notes on her doorstep. She radiated energy, always smiling, making everyone around her laugh.

He was older, felt more sophisticated. He had already been to Europe. He had even studied literature briefly at the Sorbonne. Hardly anyone did that in 1964. He thought that she would be impressed. She was just a first-year student at the university. What could she know? How could she not be impressed?

But she didn't fawn over him the way the other girls did. Quite the opposite. She ignored him. Walked right by him in the middle of a circle of friends, holding her books in front of her, her hair pulled high in a ponytail. After they walked past him, her friends huddled around her, whispering and giggling. His face burned, with embarrassment and pleasure.

One day, she boldly marched up to him when he was standing by the university gate.

"Take this," she said in a firm, confident voice, thrusting her books into his chest. He followed her, all the way to her parents' house, struggling under the weight of the books and trying to keep up with her fast pace. She stopped at her front door and waited for him. He was panting and out of breath.

She reached out and took the books from him.

"See you tomorrow," she said, and shut the door in his face.

He took her to the big spring dance. She wore a white dress with pink flowers and a matching flower in her hair. He was a good dancer. He had been told this many times and he was anxious to show off, anxious to twirl his partner around the dance floor. But she was hesitant, nervously smiling and telling him, *No, I don't really know how to dance . . .*

"I'll teach you," he said.

"Everybody will see us," she said shyly, "I will embarrass you."

His heart went out to her, she who was usually so confident, bold even! It was the first time that he sensed her vulnerability, the first time that she had shown that she, too, could feel awkward.

"You won't embarrass me," he said. "You could never embarrass me."

He took her out onto the dance floor. He put one hand firmly on her waist and the other behind her neck — she felt so small — and tried to coax her into moving her feet.

"It's easy. Just let me lead," he murmured. And then, he bent toward her and kissed her on the lips.

Her feet stopped moving. He kissed her again. He gently moved her toward him, then backward, then forward again, and she followed.

"You're doing it," he told her, "you're a good dancer."

She beamed.

"You're a good teacher," she said.

Then he was twirling her around the dance floor. She felt so light in his arms, so graceful, the white dress with the pink flowers swirling around her shapely legs, her beautiful legs, and she leaned her head back and laughed, a high pitched, excited laugh, laughing at nothing but her own happiness. He pulled her toward him and held her against his chest, in his arms, never wanting to let her go.

He fell in love with her spirit, not just her face. He felt lucky, for the spirit, he thought, remains constant. His love would remain constant, too. But when he sees his wife now, her mouth so grim, her eyes so worried, he realizes that the spirit can change. It can bend, and even break.

He closes his eyes, listening to his wife breathe, deep and even.

He had been warned. He had been told that this marriage would never last, that it would be nothing but bad luck.

His mother had walked into his room one day after he had told her about his plans to marry. She had sat on the edge of his bed with that tender look that meant she was about to tell him something he wouldn't like.

"Son," she said, "my darling son. I went to the Fortune Teller today."

He waited.

"You cannot marry."

He looked amused, white teeth showing as he smiled confidently.

"Never?" he asked.

"No, you must not marry the one you have chosen. It is not a good match. It will bring you bad luck."

"You can't tell me who to marry," he replied firmly. He had never talked back to his mother before.

"The Fortune Teller, she knows! She said terrible things!"

She grabbed her son, both hands gripping his shoulders, looking directly into his eyes. Yung Chul jerked away from her.

"What did that old lady say?" he asked. His curiosity would prove to be fatal.

"She said you and your wife will end by hating each other! She said that you will only have one child! And it will be a girl! She said that your wife will make you miserable!"

"Get out!" he told her. It was the first time that he had raised his voice at his mother. His own mother!

57

She looked at him, her eyes filled with tears. Already the Fortune Teller was right.

But he had disregarded her warning with the recklessness of love, and clung to hope with the stubbornness of youth.

Now, his mother's presence is straining the already tenuous threads holding his marriage together. He notices the way his wife avoids looking at him. He hears the sound of her voice to her daughters, to him, tinged with impatience, irritation.

He no longer has the courage to ask her what she is thinking, too afraid to hear what she might say. Better to leave the unspoken alone, he reasons, store it in a cupboard, wait for her to do something with it, the way she decides what to do with the boxes in the garage, the toys in the attic, the letters in the drawers. He waits for her to decide, waits for the moment when she will march right up to him and thrust her unhappiness into his hands and tell him, *"Take this,"* with the commanding voice that she used the first time she spoke to him, the first words being the last that he hears from her, before she turns and walks away from him, this time, forever.

Chapter 9

It is Saturday morning, and Myung Hee is sitting in front of the vanity in the bedroom, plucking gray hairs from her head. Her husband is sitting on the bed watching a rerun of "Dragnet." Chinhominey has been with them only one week, but it feels much longer.

"Owww!" Myung Hee plucks out another gray hair. "Your mother is not happy. She doesn't do anything all day!

From the television *"We caught them trying to flush two bags of weed down the toilet."*

"She does nothing but complain. The coffee's too cold. The fruit is sour."

"Where is your daughter, Kirkpatrick?"

"She watches television all day. Owww!"

"Just leave me alone! Do you have a warrant to search my house?"

Yung Chul leans over and turns up the volume. Myung Hee sighs softly, but her husband does not hear her. When did she become so unimportant? She used to be the center of his universe, the reason for his existence. He used to tell her so, promising her that he would buy her things, a diamond ring, a new car, a fur coat. She laughed, *A fur coat!*

We live in Los Angeles! She didn't want any of those things, but she liked it that he wanted them for her. It was proof, wasn't it, that he loved her, that he would do anything for her. He spent long hours at the office, working overtime to buy his wife presents. His work schedule became busier, his thoughts preoccupied with financial worries, so that when he came home, he no longer seemed to have any energy left for her.

The harder he worked, the lonelier she became, spending her days shopping, buying things, not because she wanted them, but just to pass the time. Yung Chul seemed to have forgotten about their dream of starting a small business together. He was too wrapped up in his own goals, so that when she asked him what he thought if she offered piano lessons, he merely nodded his head, told her it was a good idea. And she tried, for a few months, teaching kids how to play scales and Frère Jacques on a rented upright while her own children played quietly in the backyard. For several months, she gave lessons to girls from Beverly Hills who snapped their gum as she counted, *One, two, three*. This was not the reason we came to America, she thought, as these spoiled brats blew bubbles in her face, even as she was telling them to keep their wrists straight, to press the keys lightly, to try and try again. *Staccato, allegro, moderato*. "What did you say?" they asked in their whining voices, lacking respect, full of confidence. "I can't understand what you're saying." She stopped giving lessons, hoping that her husband would ask her why, understand her reasons, *listen* to her. Perhaps then, he would remember. But he never said anything, didn't even seem to care. The piano sat in the corner, silently gathering dust, until finally she called the rental company and had it taken away.

"Call the coroner's office. We found her!"

Christina walks into the room. She is wearing pressed khaki shorts and a crisp white sleeveless cotton shirt.

"I'm going to the beach," she says. She looks at the television and starts to laugh. Sergeant Friday is dressed in a wide-lapel suit with a wide tie. He is escorting two bad guys — hippies dressed in love beads, long hair, headbands, and striped bell bottom pants.

"Look at that hair! And those beads." She howls with laughter, "Grace! Come here, quick!"

"Sssshhh . . ." Yung Chul says, leaning closer to the television. He is not really annoyed. In fact, he rather enjoys having the entire family together. Grace comes running into the room in Guatemalan print shorts and a black tank top.

"What happened?"

"Look at that," Christina says pointing to the television, "It's so . . . retro!"

"Let's go."

"I always told Kristy, don't get too high, babe. Don't get too high. But she didn't listen to me."

"Did you hear that?" Grace asks, "He said, 'high'! He actually used that word. It's so seventies!"

"Ssshhhh!" Yung Chul says, but his daughters know that he doesn't really mean it. He still talks to them the way he used to when they were noisy young girls.

"The problem is, she did listen to you. She heard you say that grass was good for the soul."

"He said grass! He said grass instead of dope! Can you believe it? They really talked like that in those days!"

"What is so funny?" Yung Chul asks. He is glad that

they are enjoying themselves even if he doesn't understand what they find so amusing.

"Did you see that hair? It was so long and stringy!"

"And those pants!"

"They're just crazy sometimes," Myung Hee says calmly from the vanity. "Owww!"

Chinhominey walks into the room. "An old lady can't even sleep in this house," she complains.

"I see your mother has wakened from her long nap," Myung Hee remarks. She turns back to her reflection and searches for more gray hair. The smile disappears from Yung Chul's face, and he turns the volume down on the television. Christina scrambles to her feet, not wanting to hear another lecture on ill-behaved American children.

"I've got to run. Henry is coming to pick me up."

Grace, too, jumps to her feet.

"And I've got to study for class."

"It's too hot in here. Why is it so hot?" Chinhominey asks. "It's never this hot in the fall in Korea. It's the middle of September. It should be much cooler."

"It's Los Angeles. It's always hot," Myung Hee says, without turning around. She finds another wiry silver strand and yanks hard.

"I'm going for a walk," Chinhominey says.

Yung Chul glances over at his wife, his unhappy expression reflected in the mirror. Myung Hee wraps the thick gray strand of hair around her finger. The blood bulges purple against her skin as she pulls the strand tighter around her flesh.

It was raining the first time Myung Hee met her future mother-in-law. She followed Yung Chul up a muddy road to a modest house with a red-tiled sloping roof. They took off their shoes and shook the water from their raincoats. Yung Chul slid the door open, calling out to his mother. He had been so reluctant about introducing his fiancée to his mother, Myung Hee suspected there must be something wrong with her. Perhaps she was hideously ugly, or monstrously deformed. Myung Hee was surprised when she finally saw the woman who entered the room where they stood in their stockinged feet.

Yung Chul's mother was tall for a Korean woman of her age, and attractive for a woman of any age. She wore a Western-style red silk skirt with abalone shell buttons. She had thick black hair, like her son's, which fell to her shoulders, and thick black eyebrows that curved into expressive C's. She did not look like the mother of a twenty-three-year-old man. Myung Hee bowed deeply in greeting. The other woman turned to her son and asked him whether he would like some tea. Yung Chul turned to his fiancée and replied, "Myung Hee, would you like some tea?"

Without waiting for her answer, Yung Chul's mother went into the kitchen. Myung Hee whispered, "Did I do anything wrong?"

Yung Chul shook his head and kissed her on the tip of her nose.

"No, darling. She is peculiar. Still, she is my mother."

Yung Chul's mother returned with a pot of corn tea and two tea cups. She placed them on a small lacquered table in the middle of the room and sat down on the straw floor mat. Yung Chul and Myung Hee sat down next to each other on the other side of the table from her. Yung Chul's mother poured the steaming corn tea into the tea cups.

"*Uhmuhnim*," Myung Hee said hesitantly, "You did

not have to go through the trouble of making tea if you did not want to have any. We did not mean to bother you."

The other woman looked her straight in the eyes for the first time, and Myung Hee politely turned her gaze downward. Yung Chul's mother picked up one of the two tea cups and sipped from it. Myung Hee blushed, and her eyes filled with tears of embarrassment and confusion which she quickly blinked away.

Yung Chul picked up the remaining tea cup and handed it to his fiancée, who shook her head.

"Your mother made it for you," Myung Hee protested.

"If she made it for me," Yung Chul said, looking at his mother with unblinking eyes, "then it is for you. From now on, what is mine belongs to you."

He held the tea cup out to his fiancée with both hands. Myung Hee took the cup from him. She breathed in the warm corn smell and made a sipping sound, although she did not actually drink. She handed the cup back to her fiancée. Yung Chul, still glaring at his mother, took a sip from the same tea cup. His mother turned her head away in disgust. Finally, she stood up and walked into the kitchen. In a few minutes, she returned with a tea cup for her future daughter-in-law.

It wasn't until several months after they were married, that Myung Hee learned the reason for her mother-in-law's strange behavior.

It was still morning but Yung Chul was already at work at National Korea Bank where he was an apprentice. Myung Hee was reading the newspaper at the kitchen table when she heard clattering outside. She turned her head as the door opened, and Chinhominey rushed inside, still wearing her shoes! Her hair, usually combed and shining, was windblown and sticking up in places. Her coat was slipping off her shoulders.

"You must leave immediately!" she cried. "Your marriage is doomed!"

She began pulling at Myung Hee's arm. Myung Hee worried that her mother-in-law was not well. She stood up, legs trembling, and managed to extricate her arm from the other woman's hands.

"Why do you say such a thing?" Myung Hee asked, staring wide-eyed at her mother-in-law, who continued shaking her head.

"I went to see the Fortune Teller," her mother-in-law announced.

Myung Hee closed her eyes. The lights above her swirled and the sour taste of bile crept into her mouth. She gripped the edges of the table to hold onto something.

"Foolish me, I went hoping that something had changed. As if you could change fate! Great tragedy will befall my son if you stay with him. I tried to tell him, but he is so stubborn and foolish. You must not be so selfish — you must think of him!"

There was a loud crash as Myung Hee fainted, banging her head against the kitchen table. Chinhominey was too late. Myung Hee was already pregnant.

Chapter 10

Outside, Christina is sitting on the front steps, smoothing sunblock on her arms and scanning the street for Henry's blue BMW. Chinhominey walks out the front door carrying a pink and purple parasol.

"Where are you going?" Christina asks. She points to the parasol. "What's that for?"

Chinhominey looks puzzled for a moment and then looks up at the sky.

"It's not going to rain!" Christina says.

Chinhominey looks puzzled.

In broken Korean, Christina says, "No rain. Not rain."

Chinhominey makes a sharp hacking noise that sounds like a cough, but is actually a laugh.

"For sun," Chinhominey replies. "Too bright."

"You don't need to carry an umbrella," Christina says. Chinhominey nods.

"No," Christina says, "use this."

She gets up and walks over to Chinhominey, carrying her bottle of suntan lotion.

"Here," she says. She squirts some lotion into the palm of her hand. Chinhominey watches her curiously.

"For face," Christina says."

Chinhominey nods her head. Christina dabs a little lotion onto her face.

"You try it," she says, holding out her hand. Chinhominey tentatively wipes white stripes of lotion onto her face.

"Here," Christina says, rubbing the SPF 15 into her grandmother's wrinkled skin.

Christina points to the parasol.

"You don't need it," Christina says, "not necessary."

Chinhominey smiles and nods, handing the parasol to Christina. She walks stiff-legged down the street.

Christina puts the parasol into the house just as Henry pulls his BMW into the driveway. Christina sighs, relieved. Two minutes earlier and Henry would have seen her grandmother walking down the street with a parasol. He would have thought she was crazy! Henry is judgmental about certain things — food that isn't properly cooked, people who aren't smart enough, clothes that aren't well-made. When Michelle, their mutual friend, introduced them, she told Christina, "He's a perfectionist, and you're perfect." On their first date, he took her to an expensive French restaurant, speaking French to the waiter. He knew what wine to order, stood up when she went to the ladies room, and looked into her eyes when she talked. Her parents would like Henry, she knew.

Henry leans over and opens the door.

"Is that old lady your granny?" he asks. He is wearing pressed khaki shorts, similar to her own, and a white polo shirt.

"Yes," Christina says, giving him a peck on his clean-shaven cheek. She breathes in his expensive aftershave. She is glad that he is the type of man who bothers to shave even though it is a Saturday morning and they are just going to the beach.

He looks at her, his eyes scanning her flawless complexion, puts the car in reverse and backs out of the driveway. On the way down the street, they pass Chinhominey. She is taking a rest, crouched on her haunches, her face beet red.

"That's not a very ladylike way to sit," Henry remarks.

"Korean old ladies always sit like that," Christina says. She looks at her right hand. The emerald ring looks nice on her slender, carefully manicured fingers.

"It looks scary," Henry adds.

"She's not so bad," Christina says.

"I didn't say she was bad. I just said that she was sitting in a scary way," Henry snaps.

"Henry," Christina says, "I didn't mean to upset you."

Her voice is apologetic, but her hands are now grasping each other so tightly that the ring presses painfully against her fingers.

Henry turns to her with a suddenness that causes her to jump. "You're always trying to pick a fight. What's the matter with you?"

"Please, Henry," she says, turning her eyes to the road, hoping that he will do the same. "Let's just go to the beach."

"We're not going to the beach," he says, shaking his head. "I didn't want to go in the first place. It was *your* idea."

Christina stifles an exasperated sigh. "Then where are we going?"

"I don't know," Henry says. After a moment, he shakes

his head, suddenly apologetic, and wipes at his eyes with the back of his hand, "You know, honey, I'm exhausted. They have me on this rotation, and I haven't had any time to sleep."

Poor Henry. He's just tired.

"You can nap on the beach?" Christina suggests.

Henry frowns slightly. "It's too hot. I'll never fall asleep. I shouldn't have agreed to go to the beach this afternoon. I should have just taken the day to catch up on my sleep. But I've been feeling guilty, honey, because I've been working so hard. I feel like I've been neglecting you."

He reaches over and holds her left hand. Christina puts her right hand on top of his.

"The ring is beautiful," she tells him, glancing down at her right hand.

"Thank you," he says, "but I can't just buy you things. I need to spend time with you. I don't want to be like some of these guys I see at the hospital, driving around in their fancy cars, on their second and third wives. I don't want you to be like their wives, covered in jewelry, reeking of alcohol."

Christina nods absently. She hardly ever drinks. She wouldn't start just because she married Henry. She would make certain that their marriage was a success. Would she quit her job at Wilbur Elementary? She loves the kids, but it would be difficult to continue working and raise her own family. Her family would have to be her first priority. Besides, she wouldn't need to work. Henry would take care of them.

"Do you want to go home and take a nap?" she asks.

Henry shrugs.

"But *you* don't want to do that, do you?" he asks.

"Sure. Let's do that. You'll feel better after you get some sleep." *Don't be selfish,* Christina thinks, although it's a beautiful day. She was looking forward to being outside.

"I'm sorry about snapping at you," he says, reaching over and taking her hand. "I'm just tired."

"I'm sorry I snapped at *you,*" she says.

She presses the button and the window glides down. She sticks her head out, trying to get some fresh air. But they are going too fast and the rush of the wind is suffocating. She leans against the leather headrest and closes her eyes.

Chapter 11

Chinhominey walks into the house, her face as red as a strawberry.

"What happened to your face?" Myung Hee asks.

"It's hot outside," Chinhominey snaps. "My face is red because it's so hot."

She walks into the bathroom and shuts the door. Myung Hee hears a yelp and then the door opens.

"What's the matter with my face?" Chinhominey asks, pressing her hands against her cheeks. "My face looks like a baboon's bottom! It's your daughter's fault."

"My daughter is to blame for the color of your face?"

"She put sticky lotion on my face and took away my parasol."

Myung Hee marches upstairs to Grace's bedroom. She opens the door without knocking.

"What is that sticky lotion you put all over your grand-mother's face? How can you do that to your own grand-mother?" Myung Hee says, "She will complain for weeks now! Years! I won't stop hearing her complain until the day she dies!"

She stomps angrily down the stairs before Grace has a

chance to respond. Chinhominey is sitting on the couch in the living room, staring out the window and shaking her head. Myung Hee takes a deep, calming breath and lightens her step. She hopes that her mother-in-law hasn't heard her yell at Grace.

"I know that I was right to stay away for twenty years."

"You should have stayed away for twenty more," Myung Hee mutters in English.

Yung Chul walks downstairs, just in time to hear his mother say, "She acts as though I came all this way to visit *her*." She is speaking to nobody in particular.

"Believe me, I know that you would never waste a cent to come and see me," Myung Hee says.

"For once, you are right. I didn't come here to see you. I didn't even come to see my only son who you stole from me! I came to see my granddaughter."

Myung Hee laughs derisively. "Your granddaughters! The ones you warned me not to have!"

"I did not say I came to see my granddaughters. I came to see my granddaughter. The one without luck. I came to see her before I lose my opportunity. Before the prediction comes true . . ."

Grace walks downstairs. "What is going on here?" she asks. "I can't even study."

The others look at her and suddenly fall silent.

"Okay, okay, just asking," Grace says. She catches sight of Chinhominey's face, a rash developing across her forehead and cheeks. "What happened to Chinhominey's face? It's all red!"

Chinhominey touches her forehead self-consciously. She asks Myung Hee, "Did she eat lunch? Where is she going?"

"Where you going?" Myung Hee asks Grace.

"To school. I'm going to study in the library."

"Be careful," Myung Hee warns, "Drive very, very carefully."

"You should not let her go without eating lunch," Chinhominey says. "It's not healthy. She might get sick. You must be careful with her. The odds are against her."

Myung Hee tries to shake her mother-in-law's words out of her head but they infest her thinking, chewing away like termites at the foundation of her consciousness. Everything Chinhominey says runs counter to common sense. No facts to bolster her predictions. No evidence to support her conclusions. But Chinhominey's words are seductive, alluring. Even more so than before Chinhominey came to visit, Grace's very existence has become a burden, a source of anxiety for Myung Hee. Each day she wonders whether today will be *the* day. When she opens her daughter's bedroom door, will she find Grace lying in bed, pale as a ghost, cold as a block of ice? Or will the phone ring and a strange voice tell her that her daughter has been murdered, or killed in a car accident? There are so many ways to die! Ever since her mother-in-law's arrival, Myung Hee has felt that the sand is running out of the hour glass; it is almost time. Grace's destiny is linked to her grandmother's. She will die young! She will die before her own mother!

Myung Hee presses her hands against her ears but the words are coming from within, unwelcome visitors in the household of her thoughts.

"You look as terrible as I feel," Chinhominey remarks. "I am going to rest." Myung Hee notices that there are dark circles under Chinhominey's eyes. As she watches her mother-in-law make her way slowly up the stairs, she wonders if Chinhominey is ill. Maybe this is the real reason that she has come to visit. Maybe she wanted to see her family once more before she dies. And if she should die, what would happen to Grace?

Chapter 12

The following morning, Myung Hee is showing her mother-in-law the new refrigerator.

"All digital," she says proudly, pointing to the temperature display.

"Why do you need a digital display?" Chinhominey asks.

"More modern that way," Myung Hee replies. After yesterday, she has resolved not to poison her home with any more angry words.

"Refrigerator is very nice," Chinhominey says.

Myung Hee is pleased. Could it be that her mother-in-law feels as guilty as she does about their behavior of the day before?

"Would you like something to drink?" Myung Hee asks. "Some freshly squeezed orange juice? We have a juicer." She pulls the Juice Man out from underneath the counter.

"So large," Chinhominey says.

"This makes freshly squeezed juice. Delicious. So fresh," Myung Hee says. She takes several peeled oranges out of the refrigerator.

Chinhominey watches her intently. "You already peeled them?"

"This morning," Myung Hee says.

Chinhominey is unhappy. Her lower lip protrudes and her eyes turn down at the corners. Myung Hee reminds herself that Chinhominey visits only once every twenty years. She puts the peeled oranges back in the refrigerator and takes out several unpeeled oranges. It is a small concession for peace.

"You will like the juice machine," she says, as she starts to peel an orange. "So fresh. You won't believe it."

Chinhominey nods but looks a bit skeptical. Yung Chul comes downstairs dressed in plaid slacks and a polo shirt. He tries to sneak towards the garage.

"Where are you going, husband?"

"To hit a couple of buckets," he replies.

"Do you want some freshly squeezed orange juice first?" she asks.

"No," he answers and slips out the door.

"My son likes to play golf?" Chinhominey asks.

Myung Hee nods.

"It is a game that he learned after he left Korea," Chinhominey remarks. "He used to say he could never understand Korean men who played golf all the time. He said the sport seemed so boring."

"The golf courses are better here," Myung Hee explains.

"He refused to go even to the best golf course in Korea. He liked to do other things. He liked to read books. He liked to chase girls. And then, after he met you, he liked to spend time with you."

Myung Hee nods her head thoughtfully. "He liked to go for walks with me," she says, wistfully.

"He liked to sing you songs," Chinhominey says, also nodding.

"He liked to tell me stories."

"He liked to talk to you."

"He spent hours, telling me about nothing."

"His eyes were different then."

"Always bright and shining."

"Always looking at you."

Myung Hee puts the peeled orange slices into the juice machine and catches the juice in a tall glass. She hands the glass to her mother-in-law.

"So many oranges for so little juice," Chinhominey remarks. She lifts the glass to her lips and swallowing, makes a face.

"How is your juice?"

"Delicious," Chinhominey says. She sets the empty glass down on the countertop but can't help adding, "A little sour."

"It's not the season for oranges," Myung Hee says.

Christina walks into the kitchen and opens the refrigerator.

"Christina, you forgot to greet your grandmother."

"Anyonghasayo," Christina says, turning reluctantly toward her grandmother. Her eyes are puffy and red, her complexion pale.

Chinhominey points to the rash on her own face and smiles.

"Red," she says in Korean.

Christina nods, "Yes. Red."

Chinhominey points to the ceiling.

"From the sun?" Christina asks.

Her grandmother smiles and nods.

"You have a nice time with Henry last night?" Myung Hee asks.

Christina shrugs her shoulders and takes a long sip of orange juice, disguising a shuddering sigh as a slurp.

"Did you see your grandmother's face? All red!" Myung Hee says, turning to Chinhominey.

"What happened?"

"Grace put suntan lotion all over your grandmother's face and she got allergic reaction."

"That's an allergic reaction to sunscreen?" Christina asks, staring at her grandmother.

Myung Hee nods. "Can you believe it? All Grace's fault."

"Grace didn't do it. I did," Christina says, turning to her mother.

"You did?"

"I was afraid that she would get sunburned."

Myung Hee laughs, "Your grandmother has been alive for many years. You think she doesn't know how to protect herself from a sunburn?" Christina shrugs and walks upstairs.

"You want more orange juice?" Myung Hee asks her mother-in-law. Chinhominey shakes her head. "What's the matter with your daughter?"

"What are you talking about?"

"Why was she crying?"

"I didn't see any tears. You see unhappiness everywhere you look."

"And you don't see unhappiness even when you are staring it in the eyes."

"Oh you are so wise, aren't you? You don't want to see that you were wrong in your predictions! Your sour words were the product of your own desires!"

The front door opens, but neither woman hears it. Yung Chul walks wearily into the kitchen, his face ruddy from the sun, his thinning hair plastered to his forehead from his golf cap. He shakes his head sadly. These two bicker like ill-mannered children. If it were someone else's family, it might be funny. Can't they see how similar they are? Each so stubborn and unable to hold her tongue. Each so hot-tempered and refusing to listen to the other. He sighs loudly and shakes his head.

"You're supposed to be playing golf," Myung Hee says sharply.

"The course was crowded. No play time left."

Maybe Chinhominey was right, Myung Hee thinks. Maybe she *had* made a mistake marrying Yung Chul. Lots of boys were interested in her at Seoul University. Maybe one of them would have been more suitable. She tries to remember the names of these past suitors, what they looked like, the good times she had with them, but they meld together, unimpressive, none eliciting a fond recollection.

"Why do you always fight with my mother?" Yung Chul asks. "She's an old lady. She's sixty-four years old." He is counting the Korean way, including the nine months in the womb as one year.

"Only sixty-three years old American age."

"Anyway, she's old."

"You would fight with her, too, if you had to spend all

79

day listening to her talk about the bad luck that will happen to Grace. Talking about how Grace will die soon!"

"Nonsense!" Yung Chul says angrily.

"That is what she says. Every day, she tells me that is the reason why she is here, to see her granddaughter before she dies!"

"Grace is not going to die," Yung Chul says firmly, staring at his wife. Myung Hee looks down at the floor, regretful. She raises her head and looks at her husband, tears filling her eyes.

"I think your mother is sick," she says in English so that Chinhominey can't understand her.

"She is not sick. She only speaks without thinking."

Myung Hee shakes her head. "No. I think she may be truly sick. I think she may die!"

"How can you say such things?"

"Why else does she come here? After all these years? She is sick. If she dies, Grace will die!"

"Grace is going to die?"

Christina is standing in the kitchen doorway, her eyebrows furrowed with concern above her puffy eyes.

"Who says that?" Myung Hee asks.

"You guys just said that."

"Christina, don't call your parents 'you guys.' "

"Does Grace have a disease?"

"This is all Chinhominey's fault," Myung Hee says, and eyes her husband.

"Did she give Grace the disease?" Christina asks.

"Hyack! That's enough! Now you mind your own business," Yung Chul snaps.

"This is my own business. It has to do with my sister, doesn't it? And if it's a hereditary disease then I want to know about it. I could have it, too. Or it could affect my kids."

"There is no disease! How many times I have to tell you that?"

"Then why do you keep saying that Grace is going to die?"

"Grace is not going to die! The next person that says that I will chase out of this house." Yung Chul stamps his foot as though he means it.

"You will be chasing your own mother," Myung Hee says.

The front door opens, and Grace walks into the house.

"The library was closed," she says, "Some construction."

"Hi, Grace," Christina says solicitously.

"Hi," Grace says, looking at her suspiciously.

"How are you feeling?"

"Fine. Why do you ask?"

"No reason. That shirt looks very nice on you."

Grace looks down at herself. "It's the one you gave me. Do you want it back?"

"No, of course not. It's yours. If you want to borrow anything else from my closet, go right ahead."

Christina smiles gently at her younger sister. Grace looks at her, puzzled.

"Is Christina feeling okay?" she asks her mother.

"Yes! She has no disease!" her mother snaps. "Nobody has a disease!"

"Okay, fine, I was just asking," Grace says. She turns and jogs up the stairs.

"Don't run!" her mother cries. "You could fall and hurt yourself!"

Chapter 13

I can hear my son and his wife arguing downstairs. They are arguing because of me, because of the words that I cannot keep from speaking. Mothers should not always tell their children the truth. I know that as well as I know the emptiness inside me.

I might have been a better mother if I had loved my husband less. Maybe then the Fortune Teller's prophesy would not have mattered so much. Maybe then, I would have been able to forget.

But when I saw my husband lift his only child up in the air and hold him high above his own head, my spirit inflamed with bad feelings. And when I saw the way my son basked in my husband's adoration, my spirit roared even louder in protest.

What right had this child to take pleasure in this attention? To delight my husband, who loved him as though they were of the same flesh and blood?

Of course it was not fair for me to blame my infant son, but it was much easier than blaming myself.

So when my son reached his arms out to me, wanting me to reach down and pick him up, I scolded him.

"You're too big to be carried," I said even though he weighed less than the pillow upon which he rested his head.

I could not love this child. I would not love this child. For in doing so, I would betray my husband yet again.

I tried to stay away from him as much as possible. I did not rock him in my arms the way a mother does, I did not sing him songs to make him fall asleep.

I kept my distance. It was he who began to move toward me. First he moved like a worm, his head bobbing up and down as he inched his way toward me, but he was too slow and yet too small. He fell asleep before he made it halfway across the carpet.

He began to crawl on his hands and knees, like a tortoise, in my direction. I merely stepped over him and moved to the other side of the room.

One day when I was sitting at the table eating fruit, I felt something brush my foot. I glanced down. It was my son who, just moments earlier, had been sitting at the other side of the room.

He looked at me and smiled, as though he knew what he was doing. I could not resist. I reached out and lifted him to me. And though my arms were stiff as wood, I could feel that my heart was starting to melt.

Soon, my son was walking. His steps were unsteady, but he displayed such determination! Such persistence!

"See how he tries so hard?" my husband said, "Just to reach you."

But I was too quick for him. I moved to the left as he moved to the right. He stopped and turned, puzzled. Then he turned and started to follow me. I continued walking, straight into the other room, and shut the door behind me.

I closed my ears to the sound of his cries. I pretended

not to care. But he would not give up. Although his movements were unsteady, they were swift and soon I found him standing and swaying beside me, smiling and making strange baby noises that sounded like a simmering casserole.

Although I knew that I shouldn't, I reached down and picked up my son. He kissed me with his tiny mouth, leaving a damp mark on my cheek.

I hardened my heart and put my child back down. I would have succeeded in escaping had he not chosen that moment to speak his first word.

"Amma," he said.

I froze. I hoped that I had misunderstood.

But he said it again, "Amma."

I turned, and he was smiling, his arms reaching out to me in a triumphant gesture.

My son's first words spoke the truth that I was unwilling to accept.

I was his mother. He received life in my womb, he was of my flesh, it was my blood that flowed through his veins.

It was at that moment that I decided to accept my fate. If ever I questioned the wisdom of the Fortune Teller's words, I laid those doubts to rest. How else could I continue to love them both, my husband and my son, without first convincing myself that what I had done, what I was doing, was borne out of necessity? My choice was between posterity and virtue, therefore my decision was the right one. In fact, it was the only one.

Chapter 14

Later that afternoon, Yung Chul is perfecting his golf stroke on the living room carpet when Myung Hee and Christina return from the grocery store. The golf club makes a whooshing sound as Yung Chul swings.

"You will wear out the carpet," Myung Hee says. "There will be little bald patches on it just like on your head."

"Your mother is a comedian," Yung Chul says. His wife seems to be in a better mood than she was earlier.

"So many groceries," he says, picking up the bags that his wife has brought in. "What's for dinner?"

"I don't know. Depends on your mother."

"Let's go out to dinner tonight," he suggests as he walks toward the kitchen.

"But we just bought four bags of groceries . . ."

"That's what our big refrigerator is for," he replies. "We can go to the Chinese restaurant that just opened on Berendo," he says, feeling his wife's eyes on the back of his head.

"Okay," she says with a smile. She turns to Christina,

"You tell Grace and Chinhominey that we are going out to dinner."

"Okay," Christina says in a soft voice, "I better call Henry. I told him that I would go to the movies with him tonight."

Christina walks into her bedroom and closes the door behind her. She dials Henry's number. When he doesn't pick up the phone she tries calling him at work. He will probably be at work, even though it's Sunday.

He answers the phone, "Henry Fruzlow."

"Hi, darling."

"I'm in the middle of something. Can I call you back later?" Henry's voice is curt, the way it always is at work.

"I just wanted to tell you that I don't feel like going to the movies tonight," she says, "I think I'm coming down with something."

"I'll call you back," he snaps.

Christina replaces the receiver. It seems that lately every time she and Henry talk, they are either fighting or making up. Or worse, Christina feels that she is holding her tongue, compromising, to avoid an argument.

The phone rings.

"Hello?" she asks, her voice small and tight.

"What is this about not going to the movies?" Henry asks.

"I'm just feeling kind of . . . I don't know . . . tired."

Already she is wavering, already she feels herself weakening.

"So you don't want to go to the movies. Because you're tired. And I was looking forward to it all day," he says. "It made my day go by faster. I don't believe you're really that tired. The only thing you're tired of is me."

"Henry, don't be angry."

"I'm not angry," he says, his tone contradicting his words.

"Okay, okay," she says. "What time do you want to come by?"

"Forget it. I don't want to go to the movies."

Mandarin Gardens is part of the Hobart strip mall in Koreatown, a few miles west of downtown Los Angeles. Only a stone dragon statue at the entrance distinguishes it from the other nondescript restaurants on the block but behind the red doors, the interior borders on visual overload. One wall is painted with peaceful landscape scenes from rural China — a waterfall, children playing in a green field, boats floating on a lake — and the other wall depicts animals of the zodiac — dragons with smoking nostrils, pouncing tigers with pointy teeth, galloping horses with wild eyes. Even the rabbit looks ready to spring from the wall and attack.

The hostess seats the Choi family near the back. They wait until Chinhominey is seated first. The waiter sets a teapot and three little dishes on their table. The first dish is filled with sliced raw onions. The second is *chaichang*, a tangy, spicy black bean paste. The third dish contains kimchee.

The Chois use their chopsticks to dip the onions into the chaichang. They munch on the onions and kimchee while they wait for the waiter to take their order. Christina is the only one who is reluctant to partake in the pungent snacking because the smell of raw onions and garlic will linger on her breath for days. Henry would certainly complain. Henry doesn't like to experiment with food. He wants his noodles al dente and his fish cooked.

With her chopsticks, Christina finally reaches over and dips a small slice of onion into the chaichang. She picks up some *kimchee* and puts it into her mouth. The garlicky vinegar taste makes her mouth water. The kimchee triggers a flood of good memories, reminding her of family dinners around the small wooden table in the kitchen in their first house in Koreatown, and then the larger glass table in their second house in the Wilshire district, and now, the big oblong oak table in the dining room in West L.A. It's been a while since she's had kimchee. She chomps thoughtfully, *It's been seven months.* As long as she's been dating Henry. The smell of garlic seeped through her skin even after she had brushed and flossed and rinsed her mouth with mouthwash that was so strong it turned her lips blue. Henry refused to kiss her.

Christina helps herself to more kimchee. The acidity of the pickled cabbage makes her stomach gurgle.

"You never eat kimchee anymore," her father says.

"You must be hungry," Myung Hee says to Christina. A healthy appetite indicates a happy heart.

Her parents look pleased, ignoring Christina's eyes, sad and faraway. But Grace's vision is not clouded by expectations. She notices that her sister's posture is not as straight as usual. Her shoulders slouch, her spine curves slightly forward, her head bends downwards. Grace guesses that Henry is somehow responsible. Having never experienced Love, Real Love, True Love, herself, the problem seems obvious, the solution simple: Why doesn't she just dump him? Grace wonders, why doesn't she just get rid of the problem and get on with her life? Naively, she believes that affairs of the heart are easily resolved.

As Grace watches, her sister's eyes fill with tears, the tears roll down her cheeks, her lips close, as if trying to suppress the sound of her sobs. Her mother, chewing on raw onions, looks at Christina. The sharp flavor of the onion stinging her nostrils, that must be what is making Christina cry, she thinks. The spiciness of the pickled cabbage, the bite of the onions, that's what it is, her mother tells herself, as Christina curls her hands into fists, manages a small smile, swallows her tears, digs her fingernails deeper into skin.

The dishes arrive, one by one, at the table. First a platter of assorted seafood — slippery black sea cucumber, pink and white shrimp, chewy yellow jellyfish, and white scallop circles.

"This is good for you," Yung Chul says, lifting a wiggling piece of sea cucumber to his lips. He has not yet learned to speak to his daughters as adults, dispensing fatherly advice instead of stimulating conversational exchange.

A plate of steamed codfish in spicy garlic sauce arrives.

"House specialty," Yung Chul says, as he passes the fish to Grace. The white meat is so tender that it breaks into small pieces at the touch of a chopstick. Chinhominey watches the way her family eats, passing the plates to each other, mouths busy chewing and not talking. Chinhominey notices that when Myung Hee watches Christina, she has a slight smile on her lips. But when Myung Hee turns her gaze to Grace, her eyes narrow in anxious anticipation, as though expecting Grace to spill her glass of water, or choke

89

on a fish bone. Myung Hee doesn't pay attention to Yung Chul the way a doting Korean wife should. She doesn't fret that he isn't eating enough, doesn't replenish his tea cup. In fact, she hardly pays any attention to him at all. Chinhominey hears the way Yung Chul addresses his daughters, in English that even she recognizes is accented, imperfect. She sees the way her granddaughters nod their heads, eyes downcast, barely listening to their father. And why should they? Chinhominey can tell by the tone of his voice, by his gestures, that Yung Chul is only speaking words, lecturing his daughters as if they were still children.

The waiter brings a platter of morel mushrooms and bamboo shoots. The mushrooms are delicately flavorful with the consistency of tender abalone.

"This is the most expensive dish," Yung Chul says, tapping on the plate with his chopsticks.

Finally, there is a plate of crispy orange chicken.

"This chicken is too sweet," Grace says, with a grimace. Orange chicken is usually her favorite dish.

"That's because you compare it to the other dishes," Yung Chul says, "When you have really good dishes, you notice the bad qualities in the others."

Christina picks at the seafood platter. Her grandmother stares at her from across the table.

"Why doesn't she eat?" Chinhominey asks her daughter-in-law.

Myung Hee looks over at Christina.

"You want to order something else?" she asks. Christina smiles and shakes her head.

"Try this," Grace says, handing her sister the plate of mushrooms, "it tastes just like abalone."

Christina takes the plate from Grace. The plate slips out

of her hands, and the mushrooms slide off the plate onto the tablecloth.

"Ayyy!" Yung Chul says. "That was the best dish."

"You shouldn't drop plate so soon," Myung Hee scolds Grace.

"Oh, so it's *my* fault?" Grace asks, incredulously.

Chinhominey watches her family argue, her eyes large and observant. She makes a loud, angry "Pzzzttt!" sound. Four heads turn toward her.

"Order another dish," she tells her son in a stern voice.

"But it is so expensive," Yung Chul says, "the most expensive dish on the menu."

"Order another dish," she repeats. "More expensive to have your family fight. No mushrooms are so valuable. No matter how delicate."

When the plate of mushrooms arrives at the table, nobody reaches for it. Finally, Chinhominey reaches out with her chopsticks and puts a mushroom in her mouth.

"They are the same mushrooms," she says quizzically, "But taste is somehow different."

Chapter 15

Yung Chul often wonders whether his mother would have been different if his father had lived. Her longing for her dead husband was so palpable, so powerful, that as a child he felt his father's presence as though he were in the next room. He remembers how his mother used to pack a picnic lunch for the two of them. She packed *kim bap* and a thermos filled with corn tea into a straw basket, and they headed for a mountain with no name several miles outside of town. His mother spread a large colorful blanket on the mountaintop and the two sat, gazing at the green treetops below them. He waited for her to begin.

"Once upon a time," she started, "there was a man whose name was Jung Soo."

"Jung Soo?" he asked with excitement. "Wasn't that my father's name?"

His mother nodded, smiling, and continued, "He was a very brave and handsome man. One day, a wild tiger ran into the village that he lived in with his beautiful wife and his infant son. This tiger was the biggest, most dangerous beast that anyone had ever seen. It was ten times fiercer than any other tiger! All the villagers went to Jung Soo, begging him to protect them."

Sometimes the evil threat was an animal, sometimes man, sometimes nature. In the end, Jung Soo always sacrificed his life to protect the other villagers, to save his wife and son, but not before killing the tiger with his bare hands, or slaying the invading enemy marauders, or blowing out the forest fire with his dying breath. Her stories always demonstrated Jung Soo's bravery, his intelligence, his love for his family. Yung Chul did not remember his father who had died when he was very young, but his mother's stories provided a portrait more vivid than any memory. Her desire to remember was so strong, her tales so colorful, so descriptive, that Yung Chul could feel his father sitting next to him on the mountaintop. He listened rapturously to the story, watching his mother's eyes as they lit up with excitement, her hands moving about as she continued.

"They told him that the tiger would destroy them all if they did not sacrifice the most beautiful woman in the village. The most beautiful woman in the village was Jung Soo's wife. There was only one thing Jung Soo could do. He would not sacrifice his wife for the sake of the village, but if he did not, the tiger would destroy the entire village, including his wife, anyway. So he went out in search of the tiger, armed with only his courage as a sword and his love for his wife as a shield. He found the tiger, who roared so loudly that trees fell over. The tiger sprang, attacking Jung Soo, biting off both his ears and his nose. Jung Soo put both hands around the tiger's neck, and squeezed tighter and tighter, until he killed the tiger. The tiger was so heavy that when it collapsed on top of Jung Soo, it crushed him. The next day, the villagers found his body underneath the dead tiger and buried him on this very mountain top."

"Why does the story have to end so sadly?" Yung Chul asked, his lower lip jutting sullenly.

His mother took a deep breath and frowned slightly, as though she, too, wished for a different ending.

"It is not sad. It is a happy ending. In fact, you could not ask for a happier ending," his mother said, blinking rapidly to keep tears from falling, "Jung Soo was a hero. No man could expect to die in a more glorious way."

Yung Chul wondered why his mother lied to him, why she smiled even when her eyes were shiny with tears.

The story over, she then kissed him on top of the head, opened up the straw basket, and they had lunch on the mountaintop together.

Part II

Chapter 16

For the past nine weeks, Grace's bedroom has been Chinhominey's refuge. It is where she retreats to when she needs a break from the rest of the family. She is not used to having other people around, she has lived alone for over twenty years.

Chinhominey looks around the room which is functional yet spare, as plain and practical as her younger granddaughter. The walls are unadorned with posters or pictures. The room, though fairly large, contains only one overstuffed bookcase, a desk, and the bed. Chinhominey feels the pressure, in the center of her stomach, deeper, in her bowels, her intestines, deep inside. She sits on the edge of her bed, her granddaughter's bed, and holds the pain in her arms, leaning forward, trying to squeeze the hurt out of her body.

It won't be too long, she tells herself. She knows this, knows this better than she knows anything.

She has been so lonely. The loneliness ticked away inside her, a constant reminder of the emptiness of her life. A loneliness that wasn't like the sharp longing she felt when she was a girl and her mother left her alone or when she was a young bride and her husband went away on business. The loneliness of her youth had been painful but full of life, full of desire. The loneliness she feels in old age is empty, a soft throbbing, a resignation. It is a hollow feeling that echoes inside her, makes her feel as though she were made of wood, or stone, or nothing at all. It frightens her. It makes her afraid that maybe her daughter-in-law is right, maybe she is a mere shell casing, without sensitivity, or feeling. It creeps through her like a chill wind, seeps into her very bones, reminding her that she *is* alone, that nobody cares about her. They couldn't help hurting her. They are only mortal, after all, and mortals die, the way her husband did. Mortals wound with words, the way her only son does. Mortals are selfish and foolish and capable of abandoning you without a backward glance, leaving you alone and lonely in a way that hurt more than if you had never had anything at all, that caused more grief than if you had never known the love of a good man, or heard a child's laughter or felt his small hand in yours. Mortals could hurt you so that all you wanted to do was die, but you couldn't, you had to continue living, walking on knives and broken glass.

She thinks, *If I were selfish, if I were cold-hearted and cruel, if I received some sort of satisfaction in destroying the happiness of others, I would not have opened my mouth in warning.* What a mistake to think the mind would triumph over the heart, and that common sense could change the course of destiny. She had only succeeded in driving her family to a country that was several thousand miles, hundreds of cities, one ocean, and an eternity away. Her son has become a stranger, so old, his hair thinning so that she can see his scalp on top. Her daughter-in-law is so serious, her smile has disappeared. There was a time when a cool breeze was enough to make Myung Hee smile, when the sound of thunder was enough to make her laugh. Now, the sun is shining all the time, and her daughter-in-law does not seem to care. Her ears are deaf to the chirping of birds and her eyes blind to the blossoming of flowers. Blind to the pain suffered by her own daughters.

Oh, why were they so stubborn! Why hadn't they listened to her! Why hadn't they listened to fate!

The words still hurt. She tries not to remember them, but they bubble to the surface, and Chinhominey hears her daughter-in-law's voice, as clearly now as she did so long ago when she tried to save them from the Fortune Teller's dire predictions: *You just want to spread your unhappiness to everyone around you. So that we will be as miserable and alone as you are!* Such words coming out of a young girl's mouth!

Chinhominey had replied, "That is what the Fortune Teller has said. Not me!"

"The Fortune Teller probably knew what you wanted to hear!" Her daughter-in-law was crying, tears streaming down her pink cheeks, her arms folded across her chest.

"It is not what I want to hear!" Chinhominey protested. Such unfair attacks Such accusations!

"Your husband is dead! Your only son is married! You want him to cling to you as if he were still a small child!"

Such insolence Before she knew what she was doing, Chinhominey raised her hand and struck her daughter-in-law across the face, struck her so hard that she fell off the bed and landed on the floor. Her only son heard the screams and came running into the room. He saw his beautiful bride on the floor, crying pitifully, and gave his mother a look that told Chinhominey that he no longer loved her.

Grace was born exactly nine months later. The product of love and hate, loyalty and betrayal.

The worst part was that her daughter-in-law had been right. She may have been selfish, rude, bad-tempered and too beautiful, but she was not stupid. She could see past her mother-in-law's words, past the smiling face, right through to her soul. And she was right. Chinhominey had to admit that she had begrudged the newlyweds their happiness. She *had* resented her new daughter-in-law.

But Myung Hee was also wrong. I only wanted the best for my son. I wanted him to be happy, even more than I wished for my own happiness. If I made one mistake it was in thinking that by looking into the future I could change it.

So now she has come, thousands of miles, for the first time, to the promised land, to America. To forgive and be forgiven. And to say goodbye.

She feels it, the way animals sense an impending storm. Death is coming.

The door suddenly swings open, startling Chinhominey out of her reverie. She tries to sit up straight but the pain stabs her in the stomach, causing her to double over again.

"What's the matter?" Myung Hee asks, alarm in her voice. Chinhominey waves her away with one hand.

"Nothing. I have indigestion."

"Are you sick? Maybe you have food poisoning," Myung Hee asks, her forehead furrowed with worry.

"I am fine. Only too much salt in your cooking."

"Not too much salt. Maybe the chicken wasn't cooked long enough."

"It was cooked too long. Tasted rubbery. Too dry."

"How can it be rubbery and too dry?" Myung Hee

asks, somewhat relieved by her mother-in-law's complaint. Chinhominey couldn't be that sick and still be so nasty.

"How do I know? It's your cooking secret, not mine."

"Your face is pale."

"No, my face is too red because you irritate me."

Chinhominey remembers that as a young newlywed, Myung Hee often wore swingy dresses that showed off her shapely legs. Now, nearly everyday she shuffles around in the same faded blue housedress with loose threads hanging from the hemline, her hair unbrushed, not bothering to wear any make-up. She has stopped trying to maintain her husband's interest.

"You did not change your mind despite knowing the consequences," Chinhominey says, unable to stop the words.

"I am an American now," Myung Hee says, "I do not have to accept fate. I can think like an American. See the difference between an American movie and a Korean movie? American movies always have happy endings. In Korean movies, somebody dies at the end. In American movies, lovers are separated and then reunited. In Korean movies, lovers are together and then separated, usually by death."

"You will always be Korean. You have a Korean face."

"But I have an American mind."

Chinhominey shakes her head. "The only American thing about you is your children, and they are neither Korean nor American. But you, you are one hundred percent Korean. A stubborn, selfish Korean, but still a Korean."

Myung Hee narrows her eyes, turns her head away from her mother-in-law, her chin tilted slightly upward.

Chinhominey recognizes her daughter-in-law's disdainful look from many years earlier, but now she is weak, too weak to argue anymore. She clutches her stomach and moans, rocking back and forth to soothe the stabbing knives, deep inside.

"What's the matter?" Myung Hee asks, suspiciously. Can it be that Chinhominey is really in pain? "I have special tea for your stomach if you have a stomach ache."

"See? Always go back to Korean medicine."

"I also have Pepto-Bismol," Myung Hee adds before shutting the door.

Yung Chul is in the middle of calculating a client's extensive home office deductions when he feels someone staring at him and looks up. Bonnie Fong is standing in front of his desk, her hands folded in front of her, patiently waiting for him to finish his calculations. He wonders how long she has been watching him.

"Good morning, Mr. Choi. I'm sorry to disturb you, but I was wondering if I could go over some figures with you. When you have a moment, of course." She smiles pleasantly.

Bonnie is new to the accounting firm of Lee & Choi. He notices that she is wearing a floral print, button front dress that narrows at the waist. His daughter Christina has a similar dress.

"Your dress is very pretty," he says. Almost immediately, he regrets his compliment. Her face turns beet red and she looks down at the floor.

"Thank you," she murmurs.

At a quarter to noon, Yung Chul gets a telephone call from Larry Lee, his business partner.

"I'm still stuck at my attorney's office," Larry says, "I won't be able to make it for that new person's lunch."

"Bonnie."

"What?"

"Her name is Bonnie."

"Yeah, whatever. Anyway, I'll be here until I leave, I guess," Larry says, "I can't believe I was ever married to Rose. She wants to bleed me dry."

"Good luck," Yung Chul says and hangs up the phone, shaking his head. Larry is immature and selfish, but his English is much better than Yung Chul's, and he was educated in the United States. Larry is also a good businessman, very tough. Together, they make a good team. Yung Chul is the responsible one, the one who pays the bills and manages the office, and Larry is the charismatic one who drums up business.

Yung Chul grabs his jacket and walks over to Bonnie's cubbyhole office. She is frowning, checking her figures with those on a sheet of paper. He taps lightly on the door.

"Larry called and won't be able to make it. He's stuck at his lawyer's office trying to hammer out a divorce settlement."

"I can sympathize," she replies without elaborating.

The Italian restaurant where they will be having lunch is within walking distance of the office. It is a nice day, sunny and warm but not hot. They walk in awkward silence.

They enter the dimly lit restaurant, eyes blinking, adjusting to the darkness. The place is nearly empty.

"I wonder why this place isn't more crowded," Yung Chul remarks. "It's usually packed at this time."

"I'm sure it's good," she replies reassuringly.

The waiter takes their order. Yung Chul tries desperately to think of something to talk about. She's about the same age as his daughters, give or take a few years. What would he talk about with his daughters?

What *does* he talk about with his daughters? Yung Chul can't recall the last time he had a real conversation with either of them.

"Does your family live in Los Angeles?" he asks.

She shakes her head. "They live in Phoenix. I came out here with my husband."

Instinctively, Yung Chul glances at her left hand. She is not wearing a wedding band.

"We're going through a divorce," she explains. "It just wasn't working out. There was no point in beating my head against a brick wall for the rest of my life."

Yung Chul feels uncomfortable discussing such personal issues, especially with a woman whom he barely knows, a woman half his age! She's probably lonely, Yung Chul thinks.

"Do you have many friends in Los Angeles?" he asks.

"Not really. My husband, my ex-husband, I mean, is from around here."

Yung Chul glances around the room wondering when the food will arrive. At least then they'll have an excuse not to talk.

"I can understand what Mr. Lee must be going through."

It takes Yung Chul a moment to realize that she is talking about Larry.

"Nobody ever calls Larry Mr. Lee. He says it makes him feel old."

"And what should I call you?" she asks, "I don't think I ever learned your first name."

He prefers to be called Mr. Choi, but it would be awkward for her to address him so formally now that he has told her to call Larry by his first name. He wishes that Larry weren't so untraditional. Why did he have to try and be so . . . *cool* all the time? Why couldn't he just act his age? Only Yung Chul's former classmates and his mother call him by his first name. His adult friends call him "Choi-hyung" and his wife calls him "Husband."

"You can call me . . . Joe."

"Joe?"

"It's really not Joe," he says, "It's Yung Chul. But nobody calls me that. Joe is less awkward."

What he means by "awkward" is "familiar." Yung Chul is who he was when he was a schoolboy, back in Korea. It is who he was before he became an adult, before he became "Mister" or "Husband," or "Father." "Joe" is a name free of expectations, or assumptions. A name without a past.

Their food finally arrives. Two steaming plates of lasagna.

"It smells good. What an excellent choice, Joe," she says.

The sound of his new name spoken from her lips is strangely exciting.

Chapter 17

The late Wednesday afternoon traffic along Wilshire Boulevard is light. Christina checks her reflection in the rearview mirror, searching carefully for emerging pimples or potential wrinkles. She breathes a sigh of relief. Usually, the first place stress shows is on her face. But her skin is smooth with an almost translucent quality. Her eyes, however, are still puffy from last night's crying.

Don't think about it, she tells herself, *Try not to think about it.*

She knew something was wrong when Henry told her that he was too tired to sit through a movie. *Henry is always tired,* she thought to herself as they drove to his apartment in Century City. Henry was increasingly moody. Yet, they were perfect together, weren't they? He was cultured, intelligent, sophisticated. She couldn't be wrong about him. She *wouldn't be* wrong about him. She had already invested too much time and emotion into him, into their relationship. She had already convinced everyone — her friends, her parents — that he was perfect.

He pulled into his parking space and abruptly turned to her.

"Are you cheating on me?"

She laughed. Surely he was joking.

"Why are you laughing?" he asked. She could see his jaw muscles clench.

"It's just that the idea is so . . . ridiculous. What made you think that?" She tilted her head toward him, her eyes concerned, frown lines zig zagging across her forehead.

"Because I swear, if you are . . ." he paused ominously.

"Don't threaten me."

She was suddenly cold. *He's just tired,* she told herself again. He hasn't been sleeping much on this rotation. She shifted slightly, lifting her legs up from the vinyl seat, moving away from Henry.

"I wasn't threatening you. It's only a threat if you plan on doing it."

"Stop talking to me that way!"

His hand flew out suddenly, striking the right side of her face.

She would tell herself that the slap was as much of a surprise to him as it was to her. But it was difficult to convince herself.

Don't think about it, she tells herself. *Don't think about it.*

The traffic suddenly thickens near the intersection of La Brea and Beverly Boulevards and Christina slams on her brakes. Up ahead, she can see the orange cones and the large triangular sign: Left Lane Merge. The City of Los Angeles is at it again, tearing up the roads for no purpose other than to cause this late afternoon pile-up.

Christina signals and tries to maneuver her way into the right lane. The white Cadillac beside her speeds up, not wanting to let yet another driver cut in front of him. The driver keeps his eyes on the road, pretending not to see Christina, who is inching her way into his lane. Christina honks her horn, tries to change lanes anyway, and is almost hit by the white Cadillac. Christina swerves back into her lane.

"Fuckin' asshole!" Christina yells. The next car is kind enough to let her through, and she switches lanes, now directly behind the white Cadillac, driven by a man with glasses and a bushy moustache. He peers into the rearview mirror at her. She pulls up to his bumper, lifting her middle finger. The light turns green. "Fuck you!" she yells.

Take a deep breath. Exhale. Inhale. Exhale. The anger rolling around, bubbling inside. Inhale. Exhale. Inhale. Breathe deeply. Deep breaths. Take breaths. Take deep breaths.

Try not to think about it, she tells herself. *Don't think about it.*

Henry's apartment was on the top floor, spacious and filled with light. He didn't have much furniture, but what he had was top quality. He sat down on the white leather couch and reached for Christina's hand. Her heart was pounding. She looked down at her feet in her sandals, gleaming white, skeletal, toes curled and then down at her hands, folded in her lap. Little girl's hands, good girl, sitting straight, hands folded, obedient, waiting. How many times has she sat like this? Hands folded in her lap, head down. How many times? Sunday mornings at Wilshire Methodist Church. In class. At the dinner table. Listening to the preacher, to the teacher, to her parents. Listening. Such a good girl. So obedient. She listened so well.

"I didn't mean to . . . slap you," he finally said. She nodded her head, eyes staring straight ahead. He stroked her hand, her fingers. She pulled her hand away. He straightened up in his seat. Her head hurt, her heart ached. He turned to her, looked into her eyes for a split second, and then looked away. Looked into her eyes just long enough for her to see that he was crying.

"I'm sorry," he whispered. Then he was crying harder, as though his heart were breaking. She pulled him to her, against her, his head against her breast, stroking his hair, kissing the top of his head, wanting him to stop crying, anything to stop crying, it hurt her so!

He cried harder, louder, desperate sobs. She held him against her, comforting him.

"Sssshhhhh . . ." she murmured, into his hair, "Ssshhhh . . ."

His sobs subsided, became slower, softer, disappearing into an occasional gasp, a miserable tremble. He lifted his head, looked at her again. She tried not to feel sympathy or pity, or revulsion. But it was impossible. He was so helpless, so pathetic. So sorry.

"Henry," she said, sounding strange to herself, her voice was too calm, didn't reveal the way she felt inside, how she loved him, how she hated him, how he disgusted her, how she couldn't stand for him to touch her.

He started to stroke her, gently, softly, making her heart pound, her stomach churn. It wasn't the right moment, she was upset about the slap, didn't he understand that? Or did he think all their problems could be resolved that way? . . . kissing her neck, her lips, climbing over, climbing onto her . . . "You still love me, don't you? Don't you?" Desperately biting her lips, her neck. Tears rolling down her cheeks, but he didn't notice, didn't hear her, didn't see her.

The sound. What was that sound? That thumping? Fierce, his kisses fierce, When is a kiss not a kiss? When it's something more. Something much more. And so much less.

"I love you so much," he pleaded, "I'm so sorry. I love you so much."

She was unable to say anything, terrified by his desperation, his need for her.

Her head banging against the arm of the white leather couch. The horrible thumping sound of her blood pounding in her ears, panic rising, rising, "Please . . . Henry!"

Did he mistake her cry for passion? Is that why he didn't stop?

His blurred face above hers, the whites of his eyes, hands desperately clawing at her, not gentle the way he could be, sometimes, his mouth open, kissing her with his razor sharp mouth, his teeth hitting hers, cutting her lips, his horrible face, rising and falling, distorted through her tears.

A large bouquet of red roses is waiting for Christina at home. She opens the card. "I love you. Henry."

"Beautiful flowers. They smell so good," Myung Hee says.

"They're from Henry."

Chinhominey grunts, "It must have been a big one."

Christina, thinking that she misunderstood her grandmother, asks, "A big what?"

"A big fight," Chinhominey answers. Myung Hee frowns.

"I have to put these in water," Christina says, and carries her flowers away.

"Have you already forgotten your own silly words?" Myung Hee asks, "Christina is the one with the good fortune. She is the one who will bring happiness to her parents!"

"She may bring her parents happiness, but *she* is not happy."

"You are confusing her with her sister."

"You are confusing her with yourself."

Myung Hee looks at her mother-in-law, puzzled.

"Your happiness is not her happiness. What makes a parent happy is not always what makes the child happy. I know that from my own experience." She turns back to the television, intently watching two soap opera actors locked in an embrace.

"You can't even understand what they're saying," Myung Hee remarks quietly, her eyes on the set.

"Easier to know what they mean that way," Chinhominey replies.

Henry calls her a few minutes later.

"Thank you for the flowers," she tells him.

"Roses," he corrects her.

"I mean roses," she says. "They're beautiful."

"So are you."

Christina's eyes fill with tears.

"Honey," Henry says, his voice low and soothing, "You know I love you. I don't know what came over me last night. I didn't mean to hurt you."

Christina nods, but says nothing.

"I just haven't been myself. This rotation is killing me.

I was out of my head. I'm really, really sorry." Christina nods her head again. She picks at a hangnail, pushing the flap of skin up and then pressing it down with her thumb.

"Why are you so quiet?" Henry asks. "Is everything okay?"

"Yes," she says, "I should go now. I have to help my mom with dinner."

There is a long pause on the other end of the line. Christina starts to nibble on her hangnail, biting down on the flap of skin with her canine teeth.

"Do you realize that we've been seeing each other for almost a year now? And I've never been invited to have dinner at your house."

"I already told you how things are with my parents. They don't want guys to come over. They're old-fashioned that way."

"Is it because I'm white? If I were Korean, they'd invite me over," Henry says, sounding hurt.

"No they wouldn't. They're not like that. They don't really care that much that you're white, and they're glad that you're a doctor." Christina pulls at her hangnail with her teeth, ripping the cuticle so that it bleeds. She sucks her finger. *Funny that it doesn't even hurt,* she thinks.

"I have only met them once."

"That's just the way they are. They don't want to meet my boyfriends."

"Thanks," he says quietly, "now I'm just one of your boyfriends." He sighs.

"I'll talk to my mom tonight. I'll ask her. How about Saturday?" She puts pressure on her finger so that the blood flows around her cuticle.

"This Saturday?"

"Yeah. How does seven o'clock sound?"

"Fine. Thank you, sweetheart. It means a lot to me. I love you," he says, his voice now brisk and almost upbeat.

Christina hangs up the phone. Her finger is throbbing with pain.

Myung Hee is quietly fuming in the kitchen, washing lettuce leaves, when her daughter enters.

"Amma," Christina whispers, "what do you want me to do?"

Her mother looks up, startled. "You can wash rice."

Christina takes the rice cooker out of the cabinet.

"What did you and Henry fight about?" her mother suddenly asks.

"It wasn't a fight, really. It was . . . just an argument," Christina says, emptying four cups of rice into the inner chamber of the rice cooker.

"Why did Henry send flowers?"

"Because he's nice," Christina says, swishing water around to wash the rice.

"He has guilty feeling about something," her mother says hesitantly, carefully.

"What are you talking about?" Christina asks. She pours the cloudy water into the sink. She turns on the faucet and puts her injured finger under the running water, wincing with pain. Her mother has her back to Christina, carefully blotting the lettuce leaves with paper towels. Christina pours four cups of water into the rice cooker and presses the button.

"Why did you fight?" her mother persists. "Chin-hominey made me wonder."

Chinhominey, who is watching television in the next room, laughs.

"When is she going back home?" Christina asks. "I hope it's soon."

"Ayy! Must not talk about Chinhominey that way. But I have the same feeling, too," her mother says. They look at each other and smile in complicity.

After a few minutes, Christina says, "I was wondering whether we could invite Henry over for dinner sometime so you and Appa could meet him."

"We have already met him," her mother says, carefully, expectantly. She and Yung Chul have already made clear to their daughters that they have no interest in meeting a string of boyfriends. The only boy worth meeting is a future husband. Henry seems like a good candidate for a future husband — upper-middle class family, an Ivy League university, and a medical school degree. Christina wouldn't have to throw this one back. Myung Hee breaks into a wide grin, "You have an announcement to make?" Then quickly, "Okay, we have dinner with Henry. He takes us to fancy restaurant?" At the sight of Christina's confused, panic-stricken face, she quickly says, "Tell him fancy restaurant is not necessary. We go to Mandarin Gardens. No need for him to spend lots of money. We order only inexpensive dishes."

"That's not what I'm talking about. Why are you so *guitchana? You're* supposed to make dinner for Henry," Christina complains, "next Saturday night!"

Her mother shrugs, "Okay. We celebrate Saturday

night. Friday and Saturday night. Mandarin Gardens Friday night. Then celebration dinner Saturday night."

Christina sighs, exasperated. "There's nothing to celebrate."

"No problem. You have plenty of time to get married. Long engagement is good. Not too long, but not too short."

"I'm not getting married!" Christina cries, exasperated, "Why don't you ever listen to me?"

They hear the garage door open. When Yung Chul walks into the kitchen, Myung Hee blurts out, "Christina is getting married." Yung Chul stares at her blankly. "Henry is taking us all out to dinner on Friday night."

Yung Chul walks upstairs. His head is starting to pound. He lies down on the bed, eyes closed. He needs to relax for a few minutes before dinner. *Christina is getting married?* He rubs his temples. But she is so . . . young. She is only twenty . . . twenty-four. Already? It can't be! Twenty-four is not so young. His wife was younger when they were married. *But still, she seems young,* he thinks. Little Christina. And soon she will be married. Married to a husband who isn't Korean. Not that it bothers him. Not much. Not too much.

It isn't just that Henry's American. No, it's not just that. Although, Yung Chul admits that if he were completely honest, if Henry were Korean, he would be much more enthusiastic. He would still have mixed feelings, but the mix would be equal parts happiness and sadness. Right now, the mix was one to three, perhaps even one to four. Maybe one-eighth part regret. And maybe, just maybe, another one-sixteenth part longing. And maybe a little despair. Just a little.

But, he thinks, one-eighth regret and one-sixteenth each of despair and longing cancels out the one-fourth part happiness. Which can only mean one thing. He does not feel any happiness at the prospect of his daughter's marriage.

First he will get a son-in-law. And then, a grandchild. Grandchildren. That must be what is troubling me, he thinks. Even if Christina isn't too young to be a wife and mother, then I am certainly too young to be a father-in-law and definitely, absolutely, too young to be a grandfather! But it's more than that.

It would be nice, Yung Chul thinks, if I had grandchildren who resemble me. He would like to recognize himself in the face of his grandchild. Instead, his grandchild will resemble neither him nor his wife nor his daughter. Nor his son-in-law, for that matter.

My daughters are already so Americanized. They can barely speak Korean. When Henry enters their household, they will refrain from speaking any Korean at all. His wife will probably serve Americanized Korean dishes — watered-down kimchee, more red meat instead of squid or jellyfish or anything that is slippery and slimy and spicy. Americans, real Americans, usually don't like that kind of stuff. His grandchildren would never know what it was like to wake up on New Year's Day to the smell of *dok guk* simmering on the stove, nor would they truly understand those melodramatic Korean soap operas.

At first he spoke only Korean to his daughters. So that they would learn, so that they wouldn't forget. But his wife insisted that their children would never succeed, could never compete with the "real" American kids. So they compromised. They spoke to their children in Korean, and their daughters answered them in English. And now, look at the proud result. Now, their children speak without a trace of an accent. They even have American names. He had changed his elder daughter's name from Hyun Choon to Christina on the same day that Grace was born.

But in the process, they have forgotten. They no longer know how to speak Korean. Accustomed to being addressed in the informal manner, they never learned the honorific, the formal, polite way to address adults. So little by little, he succumbed, altering his speech, to include American words, phrases, sentences. And now, their roles are reversed, he is like the child, speaking pidgin English, broken English. He is reduced to speaking simple sentences to his daughters, sentences that never adequately conveyed feelings, thoughts never fully communicated.

Ties bind, they hold you back, they restrict. But they also anchor, keep you safe, steady.

Roots immobilize. But they also ground. When you cut ties, uproot, you free yourself, but you also cut yourself off from everything you were, and were a part of, before.

Leaving you, floating. Alone. Nothing to hold onto. Everything so unfamiliar. So foreign.

Even your own children. Especially your own children.

And their children. And their children's children. Until you disappear.

Chapter 18

It is almost ten o'clock on a rainy November night when the telephone rings. Christina, lounging on her white bedspread reading a magazine, reaches for it, expecting it to be Henry.

"It's for you," she says, puzzled. Grace takes the receiver. Christina continues flipping through the latest issue of *Gourmet*.

It's Mike.

"It's not too late, is it?"

"No. It's not even ten o'clock."

Mike pauses for a moment and then he says, "I'm dropping out of school. I'm flunking most of my classes. And Elizabeth and I . . . broke up. I can't study. I can't concentrate."

"You can't drop out!" The sharp rise in Grace's voice makes Christina turn.

"I don't have a choice. If I drop out, I can always register next term. If I flunk out, they won't let me come back."

"It's only the middle of the semester. You can still pull your grades up. I'll help you," Grace offers.

"Nobody can help me. I don't even have the energy to kill myself."

Grace notices that Christina is no longer turning the pages of her magazine. She huddles closer to the receiver, wishing she had her own room back.

"Very funny."

"You're right. I'm not even funny. Maybe I can be a janitor or something."

"Listen, don't do anything yet. Meet me at the food court at noon. And don't do anything stupid before then. At least don't turn in your drop-out forms."

"Okay."

"At noon."

Grace replaces the receiver. Christina looks at her, eyebrows raised. She puts down her magazine and picks up a hairbrush. She gathers her long dark hair to one side, brushing it to a glossy sheen.

"What's his name?"

"Why is it your business?" Grace asks.

"Does he have any older brothers or sisters? I might know them."

"He doesn't."

"Oh. An only child," Christina nods, "Interesting." She bends forward at the waist and continues brushing her hair. "Only children hate to be alone."

You think no guy would ever call me unless he was desperate, Grace thinks, *Desperate and lonely.*

Christina realizes that something she has said has upset her younger sister. But what? *When did we grow apart?* As girls, they were close, sharing the same dolls, the same friends. It was only when they got older that Grace started to avoid her. Christina attributed her sister's growing independence to sibling rivalry, to petty jealousy. But now, she wonders, maybe it *was* my fault. Maybe Grace pulled away to avoid being hurt, for hadn't Christina reveled in her good looks, her status as the favored daughter, the one who could do no wrong? She *liked* being the beautiful daughter, the popular sister, the one her parents seemed to love *more*. She could have been humble, she could have been supportive of her younger sister, bolstering her self-confidence instead of criticizing her. Maybe then she and Grace would be confidants now instead of wary roommates.

The telephone rings again. Grace picks up the receiver.

"Christina?" Henry asks.

Grace, without speaking, passes the receiver to her older sister.

"Hi sweetheart," she says, "I missed you."

Grace walks out of the room, to give her sister some privacy, and to spare herself the indignity of having to listen to more mush.

Christina, one ear pressed to the telephone receiver, examines her reflection in the mirror above her dresser as she talks on the phone to Henry. A source of anxiety, her beauty, another burden, another expectation. Another potential disappointment.

"Are you having a hard day, sweetie?" she asks as she checks for human flaws, emerging pimples, wrinkles, anything that could shatter the perfect picture.

"It's been a nightmare. I haven't slept in almost forty-eight hours. At least I'm off now. Did you talk to your parents?"

"Yes," Christina says, smoothing a line that has formed

across her forehead. Don't frown, she tells herself, you'll get wrinkles.

"And?"

"There's a misunderstanding . . ."

She twirls her finger around a long strand of hair. She thinks about Henry, the way he strokes her hair. How he loves her hair! She remembers the gentle way he touches her hair, as though he were afraid of hurting her, whispering, *It's so soft,* kissing her gently, kissing her hair . . .

"What kind of a misunderstanding?"

. . . But then she remembers the way he pulls her hair when they are making love, how tears spring to her eyes, how he doesn't notice, never notices . . .

"They want you to come over for dinner on Saturday. My mom wants to know whether you like Korean barbecue."

"Sure. You know I do. It's the only kind of Korean food that I like."

. . . the loose strands of hair on the pillow afterwards, the clumps of hair that come loose in her hand . . .

"Good," Christina says, "But there's a problem."

"They want me to bring the meat," he says.

"What?"

"For the barbecue."

"Henry! Of course not! They're not like that," Christina says, watching her face flush. He could be so gentle, sometimes, so kind . . .

"Then what is it?"

"They think you're going to take them out to dinner Friday night. At Mandarin Gardens."

"What? Did you tell them that?"

Christina stares glumly at her reflection.

"She thinks that you have an announcement to make. She thinks you want to say something. About us."

"What?"

She sighs, takes a deep breath, and then says, "She thinks that you're going to tell them that we're going to get married."

She waits for him to answer, holding her breath, expecting him to lose his temper.

"How did she . . ." He is laughing so hard that he can't continue.

"I don't know! Why don't you ask her?" Christina asks, annoyed. She scowls, causing lines to form around her mouth and eyes. She stops scowling. The lines disappear.

"I will. On Friday."

"Henry! What are you going to tell them?" she asks.

"I know this isn't the most romantic way to ask you, over the telephone, but will you marry me?"

He speaks confidently, as though he already knows the answer.

Christina's jaw drops. She catches a glimpse of her reflection, her mouth hanging open. I look so stupid, she thinks, with my mouth hanging open like that.

She hesitates for a moment before answering. *Is it just the shock?* she wonders, *Why don't I feel anything?*

"If you're serious, I will," she replies haltingly.

"You don't sound very happy," he says.

"I am," she says, her voice rising defensively, "Of course I am! I'm just surprised."

Her reflection frowns at her. *Is this what it's supposed to feel like?*

"I wanted to ask you Saturday night. But I couldn't wait."

"I'm ... so ... happy ..." she says. Her reflection attempts to smile, but the corners of her mouth tug downwards.

"I'm glad, too," Henry says, "Well, I better go now. I'm exhausted. I'll see you Friday."

"Great. I can't wait ..." she says, her voice cracking. She watches her reaction in the mirror. Her eyes stare back at her, glassy, unblinking.

Grace walks into the food court the next day, holding a lunch tray heavy with the chicken burrito special, eyes scanning the room for Mike. She sees him at a corner table, alone, drinking a soda. He is gazing out the window and doesn't see her.

"Hello. Anybody home?" she says. He turns and gives her a wan smile.

"Are you okay?"

"Yeah. Fine. I'm fine," he says.

"You don't sound fine," Grace says, "You sound depressed."

"Elizabeth told me that she wants to date other guys," he says, resentfully. "And I feel like shit." He stretches his face with his fist.

Someone calls out, "Hey Grace!"

Grace turns her head. It's Frances, from the Undergraduate Feminist Society, carrying a falafel on her tray. She is dressed in a sleeveless vintage dress with lots of costume jewelry, and wears a small gold nose ring through her left nostril. She is also completely bald.

"I didn't see you at the Fem meeting last week."

"I know, I had a midterm," Grace replies.

"Where are you sitting?"

"Well . . ." Grace quickly debates the wisdom of having Frances meet Mike and then decides that they're both adults. Isn't this what college is all about? Meeting people from backgrounds that are different from your own?

Grace sets her tray down on the table.

"I'm sitting over here."

"Some guy stole your table," Frances says, glaring at Mike.

"No, he's a friend of mine. From history lecture."

Frances takes a second look, squinting her eyes.

"Isn't that guy in a fraternity?"

"Excuse me," Mike says, "I exist."

"All fraternities should be banned by the university. They're the last bastions of institutionally sanctioned misogyny."

"Fraternities are not misogyny."

Grace takes a bite of her burrito. Guacamole plops onto her plate. "This burrito's not bad," she says. She wonders whether the meat is really chicken. She once read in the paper about a restaurant that was using neighborhood cats in its chicken dishes. She checks her burrito for cat hair.

"What's in it?" Frances asks.

"Chicken, beans and cheese, and some kind of hot sauce."

What *was* in the hot sauce? It looked kind of chunky. Tomatoes? Or something else? She had heard a rumor that someone last semester found a bandage in a food court burrito. Or was it in a burger?

"You'll be making some music tonight," Mike says.

"You are a pig!" Frances says in disgust. She stands up, "What did I expect? Of course you're a pig!"

She picks up her tray, "I'll see you later, Grace."

Grace looks at Mike and raises an eyebrow.

"Did you have to be so rude?"

"I wasn't rude. What about her?"

"She was just telling you what she thinks."

"I don't give two shits what she thinks. What the hell do I care what she thinks! She has a nose ring, for Chrissakes!" Mike frowns and then asks, "What's misogyny?"

"Women-hating."

"The guys in my frat don't hate women," he says, defensively, "In fact, it's the opposite. We love women!"

"That's just it. You lump all women together. They're interchangeable. You love all women, thereby loving no individual woman," Grace says, taking a sip of her soda. "Frances isn't so bad. You just have to get to know her. She broadened your horizons didn't she? She got your mind off Elizabeth, didn't she?"

"If you're saying I should go out with Frances or whatever her name is, you're out of your mind."

"I wasn't talking about that. Boy! Can't you see women as anything other than human beings that you can date? Besides, she would never go out with you. You're the wrong gender."

"Huh?"

"Frances is a lesbian."

Mike's jaw drops.

Grace smiles. "You have a lot to learn about women." She takes a long sip of her soda. "She's having a party tonight. You should come."

New jeans. Stretch jeans. Grace turns sideways, holding in her stomach. She turns a little more to look at her rear end in the mirror. Are those aerobic classes making a difference?

She passes her mother on her way out the door.

"You shouldn't drive around at night. It's too danger-ous."

Carjackings. A single woman like Grace is a likely target.

A calculated hit. A car bumping her from behind, sig-naling for her to pull to the side of the road.

A flat tire. Late at night. A stranger walks up to her win-dow, *Need any help, Miss?*

Grace shakes her head. No! she thinks, No! Not tonight. It's her mother's influence, making her worry about everything, always telling her to be careful, alerting her to the dangers that lurk under the bed, around the cor-ner, down the street. But not tonight. She won't let her evil negative thoughts ruin this evening. She passes a liquor store. I should bring a bottle of wine, she thinks, especially since I'm bringing someone.

Bringing someone. It has a nice ring to it.

"So you're pretty good friends with that dyke with the nose ring?" Mike asks as Grace parks the car in front of Frances' apartment.

"I don't have anything against dykes, you know. Except they won't have sex with me."

"Neither will a lot of straight women."

"Thanks. That's just what my tender ego needs at the moment."

They take the elevator to the third floor. Music pours out of the apartment at the end of the hall. Mike turns to Grace and raises his eyebrows.

"Be yourself," she says, "But with an open mind."

The living room is dark, illuminated by flickering

candles. It takes a moment for their eyes to adjust and then they can see people sitting on the floor in groups, talking softly. Music in the background reminds Grace of wailing witches at midnight, women with broken hearts, men with lost souls.

Frances rises from the floor when she sees them. She is wearing a filmy gold slip that shows off her lithe figure. A small gold chain is threaded through her nostril.

"Why is everyone sitting on the ground?" Mike asks.

"It's more intimate that way," Frances says in a whisper. "What do you want to drink? We have cognac, espresso, and wine."

"No beer?" Mike asks.

They lower themselves onto the carpet. A man seated on the floor with his back to them turns around and extends a hand.

"Hi, I'm Jerome," he says. His hair is closely shaven except for the tail in the back. Each finger is adorned with silver rings.

Grace shakes Jerome's hand, "I'm Grace."

"I know you, Grace. From Lulu."

"Lulu?" Grace asks.

"Planet Lulu. In a former life," Jerome says.

Mike groans and rolls his eyes. Grace stifles a laugh.

"You were a princess and I was your prince," he says.

Mike shakes his head, "I don't believe this guy."

"You were the court jester," Jerome tells him.

Frances returns with their drinks and joins them on the carpet. "What lies are you spinning now?" she asks Jerome.

"Lies? There are no lies. Only truths in a parallel universe."

"What has this guy been sniffing?" Mike asks.

Jerome shakes his head, "I'm high on life."

"This is the nineties," Mike replies, "Nobody gets high on life anymore." He reaches for his cognac. Grace tries not to smile. She leans over and whispers in his ear, "Free your mind. The rest will follow."

Frances murmurs, "What are you two whispering about? It's not polite."

"Everyone else in this room is whispering," Mike says.

"You're whispering in an exclusionary manner," she says, "You're being noncommunal. You're being individualistic."

Frances moves aside so they can join her group.

"What are you guys talking about?" Grace whispers.

"Pornography," Frances replies. A joint magically appears between her fingers. She takes a long drag and passes it to Jerome.

"Any supporting documents?" Mike asks. Grace elbows him.

"We're discussing whether it perpetuates violence against women."

"I think it should be outlawed," says Felicia, a woman wearing a scarf around her forehead.

Mike rolls his eyes, "Oh brother."

"On what do you base your denigration of Felicia's proposition?" Jerome asks.

"The Constitution," Mike says, simply, "Freedom of speech."

"Oh god," Felicia says, slapping her hand to her forehead.

"Once the government starts banning pornography,

they'll start banning dirty books, then books that they think are dirty, and then books that have unacceptable ideas in them. Did you think the Robert Mapplethorpe exhibit was pornographic?"

Grace watches Mike, his eyes shining, his cheeks flushed with enthusiasm. She has never seen him look so animated.

"It was art," Felicia says flatly.

"Give me a break. A picture of some guy shoving his fist up another guy's ass is art?"

Grace laughs at his blunt statement. She is surprised by his interest in this subject, in his eagerness to engage in this conversation. She wasn't quite sure, up to that moment, whether he was capable of talking about anything other than football and his ex-girlfriend.

"It was beautifully done," Frances says loftily.

"So are some pornographic movies."

"There's a difference between nudity and pornography."

"Where's the line? Who are we going to trust to make that distinction? The government?"

Frances looks at Mike angrily, her arms folded across her chest, her nostrils flaring.

"You and your free speech. You think that's the only constitutional right worth protecting."

"It's the most important one."

"Oh really?" Frances asks, "Lick my clit suck my cunt you mother fuckin' smelly prick!"

Mike's jaw drops open. "You're sick," he says.

Frances smiles, triumphantly. "What's the matter? I'm just exercising my right to expression."

Grace laughs. Mike turns to her, "You think that's funny? If I said that, you would have called me a frat boy pig. But because your friend said it, you think it's funny."

"What was really funny was the look on your face." Grace can't stop smiling even though Frances is looking at her suspiciously. Mike starts to say something, but instead, breaks into a smile. The intensity he displayed a moment earlier evaporates and his features soften as he continues looking at Grace. Grace looks away, suddenly embarrassed. At that moment she feels a zinging sensation in her stomach, like the feeling she has when a roller coaster suddenly dips.

Frances knocks back the rest of her cognac, runs over to the stereo and changes the music. She puts on loud alternative rock. She dances spastically, her small breasts jiggling neatly.

"That dress is totally see-through," Mike says.

The hard driving number changes to a slower song with comprehensible lyrics. Frances pulls Felicia close to her, and the two of them dance, cheek to cheek.

"Try not to stare," Grace whispers to Mike.

"I'm not staring," he says. He puts both hands on her waist and pulls her toward him.

"I can't slow dance," she says.

"Just let your body find the music," he whispers.

It is nearly two o'clock in the morning when they pull up in front of Mike's apartment.

"Thanks for inviting me to the party," he says, "I really did have a good time. It was interesting. You were right. I need to expand my horizons."

Mike looks straight ahead, suddenly nervous, and then

turns his eyes to her. Grace feels the same dipping zinging sensation in her stomach that she felt earlier.

"I wanted to tell you," he says, awkwardly, "But you look nice. What did you do to your hair?"

"I brushed it," she whispers, barely able to breathe. Has he always been this handsome?

Mike leans over and kisses Grace on the lips. A long, lingering, open-mouth kiss, leaving Grace gasping, longing for another.

The light is shining through the living room window. Grace opens the front door, expecting to see her mother waiting for her. Instead, her grandmother is sitting on the couch, staring up at her.

"Chinhominey," she says, surprised.

Her grandmother smiles at her and nods, relieved that her granddaughter has made it home safely. She continues staring at Grace expectantly, as though waiting for Grace to say something else.

"You hungry?" her grandmother asks. Grace shakes her head. Her grandmother wrinkles her forehead worriedly, opens her mouth as though to say something, but doesn't. She knows that Grace wouldn't understand her anyway.

"Are you hungry?" Grace asks.

"No," her grandmother replies. Grace shifts uncomfortably under her grandmother's steady gaze. *Why* is Chinhominey staring at her that way, her eyes round with concern, her lips stretched into that plastic smile? Grace feels a mixture of frustration and relief at her inability to communicate with her grandmother. It's a handy excuse to cut the conversation short, but Grace wonders what she is missing. Her grandmother seems to want desperately to speak with her.

The next morning, she is staring into a bowl of cereal.

"You came home so late last night," her mother says.

"It wasn't that late," Grace lies.

"It was so late that it was early," her mother replies.

Grace lifts a spoonful of cereal to her lips, thinking *Mike kissed me last night!*

"What are you smiling about? Why are you staring at your spoon like that?" her mother asks.

"No reason," Grace replies. Is it a crime to be happy? She shoves the spoon into her mouth and chews thoughtfully, wondering whether Mike is feeling the same nervous excitement in his stomach. He was a good kisser, his lips were soft, no thrusting tongue, no sloppy noises. Her palms sweat as she wonders what he is thinking, whether he thought that *she* was a good kisser. She vows to rub petroleum jelly into her lips every night, the way Christina does. Maybe she had bad breath. Maybe he never wants to speak with her again.

"Don't forget that we are going out to dinner tonight," her mother tells her, "Henry is taking us out to Mandarin Gardens. The whole family."

"Today's not Christina's birthday," Grace says.

"Another special day," her mother answers with a big smile. Her mother looks strange when she smiles, or maybe it's because she hasn't smiled for so long.

"Be home early. We won't wait for you," her mother says.

Chapter 19

My daughter-in-law knocks on the door while I am getting dressed. Then she walks in before I give her permission to enter.

"Grandmother," she says, "How is your stomach today?"

Today, I do not have a stomachache, but I have learned that ill health creates sympathy.

"Not so good," I tell her, shaking my head.

"Maybe you should see a doctor," she says.

"No," I reply, "if nothing is wrong, we pay lots of money for nothing. If something is wrong, we pay lots of money to hear bad news." I try to look brave.

My daughter-in-law looks at me knowing that I already pay lots of money to hear bad news. But she doesn't say anything. Maybe she is learning manners.

"I am worried about your health. Maybe you should stay home tonight," she says.

Ah! That is the reason for Myung Hee's concern.

"No, no, I feel okay. I may not die tonight," I say.

"The excitement may not be good for your digestive system," she says.

"This American boy, I am not so excited for him to meet," I tell her.

"Maybe you should stay home and rest."

"I have rested all day. I am not so tired," I say.

"The food may be too spicy for your delicate stomach," she persists.

"Then I will order only bland dishes," I tell her.

"Last time, the mushrooms were very spicy," she says. This is a lie. The mushrooms were not at all spicy.

"You do not want me to order them because they are so expensive," I tell her.

"They were not so expensive," she says. Her face turns red. My daughter-in-law is not a very good liar.

"This American boy must be very cheap," I add.

"No, he is generous. He has a good heart."

"Then it is you who are cheap for valuing a plate of mushrooms above your mother-in-law's feelings."

"I was concerned about your health," she says, "I don't care about the mushrooms. I did not think they tasted very good."

"You think they are too expensive. You do not want the American boy to have to pay for mushrooms. You think that your daughter is not even worth the price of mushrooms!"

I expect Myung Hee to march angrily out of my room the way she usually does. But she doesn't. She sits down on the edge of my bed. She looks sad. Defeated. Old. It was not so long ago that she was the most beautiful woman in Seoul. It was not so long ago that her spirit burned bright with hope.

The pain expands throughout my stomach. Rises to my chest, to my heart.

"Christina," she says, and for a moment I think that she is calling for her older daughter. But she continues, "Christina loves this boy very much." Then I realize what she is trying to tell me. She is not concerned about the price of mushrooms. She does not care if I order all the items on the menu so long as I do not take from her daughter what I had taken from her so many years ago. And I feel very, very ashamed. I am ashamed because she is so much wiser than I. I am ashamed because she is so much less selfish than I.

The pain is making it hard to breathe, rising, rising to my head. The pain pushes against my skull. I close my eyes, to contain it, so that it won't escape. So that only I can feel it.

Mandarin Gardens is crowded. A waterfall trickles down one wall into a pond with orange, red, and white koi fish. Myung Hee turns to Henry.

"Very nice restaurant," she tells him, "Good choice."

"Thank you," he replies, forgetting that it was her selection.

Henry waits until everyone else is seated before sitting down.

Yung Chul, without even looking at the menu, tells the waiter, "Mushrooms."

Myung Hee looks at her husband, annoyed. "Orange chicken," she says, closing her menu.

Grace says, "Seafood combination."

Yung Chul smiles. The seafood combination is the next most expensive item on the menu. Myung Hee shakes her head, "That doesn't taste so good. Lemon chicken is good."

"I don't want lemon chicken," Grace says, "Anyway, we already ordered one chicken dish."

Chinhominey nods her head approvingly, supporting Grace even though she doesn't understand a word she is saying. Christina looks like she wants to disappear into the fish pond.

"Your turn," Henry says. Chinhominey turns her sharp eyes on him. Henry is usurping Yung Chul's authority at the table.

"I'll have . . . the mixed vegetables in oyster sauce," Christina replies.

Henry turns to Chinhominey. Chinhominey continues staring at him, her mouth set in a grim line, her face expressionless, scrutinizing.

"She has a stomachache," Myung Hee says, "She doesn't want to eat."

Yung Chul turns to the waiter, "That's all."

"Appa!" Christina says, embarrassed, "Henry hasn't ordered!"

"I'll have the seasoned fish," Henry says.

The waiter shakes his head. "Very hot," he says. "Too hot for you."

"That's okay," Henry says, defensively, "I like hot food."

"No, no," the waiter warns, "Very hot. But we can make less hot."

"No, make it the way it's supposed to be," Henry protests, "I like spicy foods." He turns to Yung Chul. "When I was a kid, I used to put Tabasco sauce over everything."

Yung Chul is apparently fascinated by the fish pond and

pretends not to hear Henry. He wonders, *What is it about this kid that is so irritating?* He's too . . . confident. Why doesn't he feel awkward, the way a boy is supposed to when he meets his girlfriend's parents?

Grace glares at Henry. What's so great about him anyway? She doesn't see the allure. She catches Chinhominey's eyes, and they exchange glances. Her grandmother smiles briefly. Grace gets the feeling that Chinhominey isn't crazy about Henry, either.

Henry smiles at Chinhominey. She doesn't smile back. He tries his luck with Grace.

"You graduate this semester, don't you? What are you going to do after graduation?"

"I don't know . . . I applied to some graduate schools . . ."

"She's going to law school," Yung Chul says proudly. He is enamored of the female attorneys whom he sees on television. So smart and stylish! His daughter will be one of them, calmly staring down drug dealers and racketeers, fighting for justice and equality.

"She's going to Harvard," Yung Chul says confidently as though the admissions process were entirely in his hands.

"Only A's," Myung Hee adds, "Straight A's."

Grace's good grades are objective proof that she isn't a complete and utter loser. Only winners went to Harvard. If Grace got into Harvard, maybe her luck would change.

"That's great," Henry says, "although it'll be tough to get in. Even with straight A's."

Grace rolls her eyes, which makes Chinhominey smile like the grinch who stole Christmas.

The waiter brings six plates, five pairs of chopsticks and a fork for Henry.

"I hate it when they do this. Like I can't use chopsticks!" Henry says, angrily, "Reverse discrimination! And that whole bit about the fish being too hot! I'm so sick of it!"

Yung Chul turns his attention to the ceiling. Myung Hee purses her lips and inspects her chopsticks. Grace scowls and folds her arms across her chest. Chinhominey doesn't take her eyes off Henry and Christina. Why is this impudent American boy raising his voice like this?

The waiter returns with the plate of mushrooms, which he sets down in front of Henry. Chinhominey stares at Henry with watchful eyes. Henry, in a gesture of respect, passes the dish to Yung Chul first, without taking any mushrooms for himself. Yung Chul, pleased by Henry's deference, puts some mushrooms on his plate and then passes the dish back to Henry. Henry puts some mushrooms on his plate and passes the dish to Christina.

Grace whispers to Chinhominey and points to her plate. "You sure that you don't want any?"

Chinhominey lifts up one hand and shakes her head, as the rest of the dishes arrive. Soon, the table is quiet except for the clinking of chopsticks and the chomping, chewing, slurping sounds of six mouths in action. Henry sniffles. He wipes his nose with his napkin and the back of his wrist. Yung Chul reaches for a second helping of mushrooms. Chinhominey continues to stare at Henry as though he were an alien being who has just scrambled out from the fish pond.

Toward the end of the meal, Henry taps lightly on his glass with his chopsticks. The Chois all look up. The seasoned fish was a little too spicy for him. He blows his nose on the cloth napkin. Chinhominey stares at him in horrified disbelief as she dramatically places one hand across her nose and mouth. *This American boy is disgusting!* Everyone but Chinhominey puts down their chopsticks and gives Henry their full attention. Chinhominey picks up her chopsticks and starts to drum them against the tablecloth. She drums the chopsticks more quickly against the tablecloth, making a sound like rapid gunfire.

"Christina and I," Henry says with a broad smile, "Have decided to . . ."

Chinhominey knocks over her water glass. Water spreads over the tablecloth and drips onto the floor. Henry glances at the spilled water but continues talking, ". . . get married."

Myung Hee is beaming. Grace's jaw drops. Henry leans over and kisses Christina on the lips. Chinhominey shakes her head and mops up the spilled water.

"Why is your grandmother shaking her head?" Henry asks.

"I don't know. She acts weird sometimes," Grace replies, although she thinks Chinhominey's reaction is the only appropriate one. Henry is a cretin.

They are leaving the restaurant when a boy about four years old, with dark hair and fair skin, walks out of the restroom. When he sees Henry, he cries, "Daddy! Daddy!" and runs over to Henry.

"Hey there, kiddo," Henry says. He bends over and rumples the little boy's hair and then continues walking. The little boy watches him go, fists clenched, looking as though he wants to cry.

In the car in the Mandarin Gardens parking lot, Henry says to Christina, "That wasn't so bad." His face is illuminated by the streetlight. Strong jaw, firm chin, straight nose. Henry is a good looking man, Christina thinks, I should feel lucky to have him. But . . .

Henry turns a corner, "I think your dad hates it that we're getting married. I don't think he likes me. And I think he hates the idea of us getting married."

Christina glances at him out of the corner of her eye. It looks as though Henry is smiling. Why doesn't it bother him if he believes what he says? Doesn't her father's opinion matter?

"He doesn't like the idea of his darling daughter marrying some white guy."

Is it my imagination? Or does Henry look triumphant?

Christina shakes her head, "That's not true."

"Don't get me wrong," he says, turning to her. He is smiling, boldly, frighteningly, "I don't give a shit if he doesn't like it."

"You don't?"

"He'll just have to get used to the idea."

At the house, Henry pulls Christina toward him.

"It's too bad that you have to go inside," he says, "It would be great if you could stay at my place." Then, "I almost forgot." He reaches into his jacket pocket and pulls out a small black velvet box. He hands it to her.

The diamond ring is larger than she expected, although she doesn't really know what she expected. It looks like the rings she sees in magazines, a large solitaire with a gold band. It must be about two carats. Most women would be happy with one.

Myung Hee and Grace are watching television when Christina walks into the room and joins them on the couch.

Christina looks down at the black velvet box she is clutching. "Henry gave me a ring."

She hands the box to her sister. Grace stares at the diamond, unsure what to do with it.

"Big ring. Over two carats," Myung Hee says, taking the box from Grace, but she looks displeased.

"What's the matter?" Christina asks.

"Not so clean. Not so good quality. Big ring. Very big ring. But not so clear. Not the best quality," her mother murmurs, frowning slightly.

Christina takes the ring back from her mother, annoyed. Why would her mother say something like that?

She leaves the ring on her dresser, in the open box. She lies in bed, listening to the sound of Grace's deep, even breathing. She envies her younger sister. She never seems to have any problems. Grace would never do anything that she didn't want to do.

Out of the darkness, Grace asks, "Who was that little kid?"

"What little kid?" Christina asks, startled. She had thought Grace was sleeping.

"That kid who ran up to Henry," Grace says, sitting up, looking at her sister. "Remember? When we were leaving the restaurant?"

"Just some kid. I don't know. Why do you ask?" *Don't say it,* Christina thinks. *Please, don't say it.*

"There was something about the way that kid ran up to him. Like he knew him."

The whiteness of the ring gleams brightly, beckoning Christina. It twinkles in the moonlight that streams through the crack in the curtains, twinkling on her dresser like a star, like a diamond. A diamond. A big diamond. Two carats, wasn't that what her mother had said? She climbs out of bed and looks at the sparkling ring, a beacon in the darkness. It looks clear, doesn't it? Despite what her mother said? It looks like the best quality diamond from the best jewelry store in town, it does! In this light, it looks like the perfect diamond. But in this light, a piece of glass would look like the perfect diamond. Christina closes the box and returns to her bed, snuggling under the covers, her face flushed, but she is suddenly very cold, chilled, shivering. She wiggles her toes around, trying to warm her feet.

"Kids don't act like that," Grace says, watching her sister's shadowy outline.

"What do you mean?" Christina asks slowly, looking down at the blanket, refusing to look at her sister even in the darkness. But she knows what Grace means. It is what Christina herself has been thinking. There *was* something about that little boy. When Henry bent down and rumpled his hair, the little boy looked so happy! There was something about the way he looked, the way he ran over yelling, Daddy! Daddy!

"That kid knew Henry, didn't he? He's not telling the truth . . ."

142

Christina remembers the look on the little boy's face. She feels the truth in her bones of what Grace is saying.

"That little boy is Henry's son."

The phone booth smells like urine. Christina holds the receiver away from her so that it doesn't touch her ear. Grace gives her sister's shoulder a little squeeze.

"What city please?"

The operator sounds bored.

"Los Angeles," Christina replies, "Last name Fruzlow." Christina reads the graffiti etched into the glass. *Fuck you. Suck me. 450-2391. Call Rachel shes a hore!*

"There are three Fruzlows. Henry Fruzlow, Jacob, and an M. Fruzlow."

"M. Fruzlow."

"The number is 623-9045."

Ron has a small dick. Lisa has a big pussy.

Christina repeats the number aloud as she shoves a quarter into the telephone and dials. It rings once, twice, three times. Christina hands the receiver to Grace, whispering, "I can't do it." Grace shakes her head but takes the receiver just as a woman picks up the other end of the line. She sounds tired, like she was sleeping. It must be after midnight. The sky is purple, lighter in some places than in others.

"Hello, is this Ms. Fruzlow?" Grace asks in a quaking voice.

"Yes," the woman replies, cautiously, "Who is this?"

"My name is Christina Choi," Grace says, looking at her sister who is biting her lower lip.

"Do I know you?"

"No, but I think you know my fiancé," Grace says, softly, "Henry Fruzlow."

The woman on the other end is silent. Finally she asks, "What do you want?"

"I want to know the truth," Grace says, "And I'm afraid if I ask him, I won't find it."

As they had agreed, Christina and Grace arrive at the coffee shop at six o'clock the next morning. Marilyn Fruzlow is a Chinese-American woman with pale almost translucent skin. When she sees the sisters, she extends her hand in a self-consciously confident manner. Grace is surprised at the resemblance between Marilyn and her sister.

Like staring at my own reflection, Christina thinks.

"You . . . you are going to marry . . . him?" Marilyn asks, looking at Christina.

"I don't know," Christina says, "I was going to. I mean, we're engaged and everything. He even gave me a ring." She pauses, her eyes filling with tears.

Grace reaches over and hugs her sister. Christina wipes her nose with a napkin and shakes her head. She starts to cry, silently, wiping her tears away as quickly as they appear. Grace continues for her, "We were at Mandarin Gardens. Chinese restaurant on Berendo." She observes the other woman for a reaction, but Marilyn's face remains blank.

"We saw this kid . . . he came running up to us, to Henry. He acted as if he knew him. He even called him Daddy. That was his kid, wasn't it?" Grace asks.

The waitress returns with steaming mugs of coffee. Marilyn takes a long sip of hot coffee before answering.

"I saw him ... after we had already ordered, but I didn't think that Raymond would recognize him."

Her eyes fill with tears.

"It's been so long since he's seen his father. Raymond didn't understand why his father pretended not to know him. He thought it was a game. He kept waiting for Henry to come back and tell him ... ."

Grace takes a long sip of cold water, wondering, *What kind of man turns his back on his own son?*

"I wonder how long he was going to keep it from me," Christina says, finally, "That he had an ex-wife and a son."

"You don't have to marry him," Marilyn says, "It's not too late."

Chapter 20

Chinhominey and Myung Hee are making *mandoo* for tonight's dinner, even though it is not yet noon. Myung Hee has been up since seven, chopping and slicing and dicing in preparation for the big celebration dinner tonight.

"Does he come from a good family?" Chinhominey asks as she places a spoonful of the pork filling into the center of the gyoza wrapper.

"His father is a surgeon. Very famous," Myung Hee says.

"He does not have a trustworthy face," Chinhominey says. "And his ears are too small. He will not listen to his wife. He will not listen to his mother-in-law. They are small and flat. Pressed against his head."

"But, his nose is big. He will have good fortune."

Chinhominey dips her finger into the bowl of water and moistens the edges of the gyoza wrapper. She carefully presses the edges of the wrapper together.

"He has terrible manners. He blows his nose in front of everyone, without shame."

"He is an American. He doesn't realize it is bad manners."

"He is arrogant. Too proud."

"He has much to be proud of. He is a doctor. Did you notice the way he passed the mushroom dish to my husband before he served himself? Most American boys would have taken the best mushrooms for themselves."

"Good for your husband, but not for your daughter."

"What do you mean?" Myung Hee asks.

"He served himself before he served his own fiancée. Most American boys would serve their fiancée first."

"How do you know? You don't even know any American boys," Myung Hee says.

"I saw it on television. American boys treat their wives like queens. But not that boy from last night. If he does not serve his wife before they are married, how will he treat her afterwards?"

"You only see the bad things. Did you notice how he stood up and waited until everyone was seated before he sat down?"

"He was too calm. If he cared what our family thought about him, he would have been nervous. He would have spilled his drink or dropped a dish. But he was very calm. He does not care what you think about him."

"He is confident."

"He is overconfident."

"He is well-mannered."

"He becomes angry too easily. Over a pair of chopsticks."

Grace stumbles into the room and opens the cupboard. She stares, bleary-eyed, at the shelves before taking out a box of cereal.

"Christina's still sleeping!" Myung Hee exclaims.

"No she's not," Grace says, pouring cereal into a bowl.

"So much to do before dinner!" Myung Hee says.

"Dinner? It's not even noon."

"Henry is coming for dinner."

"We had dinner with him last night," Grace says, "Isn't that enough?"

She walks over to the dining room table and sits down beside her grandmother.

"Good morning, Chinhominey." Chinhominey smiles and nods almost agreeably.

Christina trudges reluctantly into the kitchen. Her hair is uncombed, unruly, her eyes puffy and swollen.

"Where have you been? I woke up early to make dinner for Henry. You should help me."

"Henry's not coming over for dinner," Christina says, her voice gruff.

"No celebration dinner?" her mother asks.

"There's nothing to celebrate," Christina says, her eyes filling with tears.

"Wedding celebration," her mother insists.

"There isn't going to be any wedding!" Christina yells. She turns and runs upstairs. Myung Hee continues spooning the pork filling into the gyoza wrapper, avoiding her mother-in-law's eyes.

The three women sit at the kitchen table, pretending nothing unusual has happened. The sound of the spoon hitting the bottom of the cereal bowl echoes like the closing of a cell door. The telephone startles them all. Myung Hee's body tenses up, on guard. Grace reaches for the phone.

It's Mike.

She covers the mouthpiece and tells her mother, "It's for me."

148

"Do you want to have dinner tonight?"

"Okay," Grace says, looking at her mother who continues to make *mandoo,* putting a spoonful of the pork filing in the gyoza wrapper, moistening the edges, closing the dumpling into neat half-circles.

Grace has never seen Mike in khaki trousers. In fact, she has never seen him wear anything but jeans and a tee shirt. But tonight he is wearing a white dress shirt with khaki trousers and brown lace-up shoes.

"Do you like sushi?" he asks. She looks at him, wondering if she heard him correctly.

"Because I know of a place. It's good," he says.

"Oh yeah?" she says, "I never knew that you liked sushi."

His face turns red. Grace has the feeling that she has somehow insulted him.

The restaurant is crowded but there are two seats at the sushi bar. Mike examines the plastic menu with the pictures of the different types of sushi. The waitress pours green tea into their tea cups. The sushi chef looks at them, ready to take their order.

"Saba," Grace says.

"Umm . . . I'll have the salmon," Mike says, "For now."

Grace takes a sip of tea and watches the chef select a piece of mackerel.

"What happened to the big family dinner?" Mike asks.

"It's cancelled,"

"Fight with the boyfriend," Mike guesses.

"Big fight," Grace adds. She separates her chopsticks and rubs them together to remove the splinters. "She found out that he was married before. He even has a kid."

149

Grace lifts a piece of sushi to her lips, using her chopsticks.

"I always thought he was a Class A asshole, but my mom practically did back flips when she found out that Christina was engaged to a doctor. I thought my dad liked him, too, at least he hasn't said anything negative. That surprised me because Henry's not Korean. I always thought they wanted us to marry Korean men. But then again, they would approve of anything that Christina did. If she married a Martian that probably would change their whole outlook on little green men. I'm the loser in the family."

"You?" Mike says, raising his eyebrows, "Little Miss Honor Roll?"

"No matter what I do, it's not good enough. But everything Christina does is perfect. You should be glad you're an only child."

Mike looks at her, his eyes soft, his expression tender, "It gets kind of lonely sometimes. It would be nice to have someone to talk to about family stuff." He reaches for another piece of sushi. It suddenly occurs to Grace that he is using his fingers because he doesn't know how to use chopsticks.

It is almost nine o'clock that evening, and Christina has not yet left her bedroom. Myung Hee hesitates, presses her ear to the door, listens, but hears nothing. She wants to open the door, but she is afraid to intrude. Her husband watches her from down the hallway. She raises her hand to knock but then lowers it.

"Did you hear anything?" her husband asks. "Did she tell you what happened?"

"Don't talk so loud," she says. "She might hear you."

"What did she say?" Yung Chul asks.

"She didn't say anything. She just told us that the wedding was cancelled," his wife says.

"What is all this whispering?" Chinhominey calls from her open door. "You sound like thieves! What are you planning to do? That is your daughter, not a stranger! If you want to know something, why don't you ask her?" She glances at her watch, "Your daughter must be hungry! It's so late! She didn't eat anything all day."

The bedroom door opens. Christina's hair is combed, gleaming and straight. She has changed her clothes and is wearing a flowered print dress.

"Why is everyone standing here?" she asks, annoyed. Her eyes are swollen, and her nose is red, but her movements are graceful and assured. She walks downstairs and into the kitchen, back straight, head held high. Chinhominey gives her son and her daughter-in-law a withering glare before marching downstairs, disdain evident in her every step.

Christina is spreading peanut butter and jam on a slice of white bread. Chinhominey stands next to her, watching. Christina points to the sandwich, "Do you want one?" She folds over the slice of bread, pressing down on the sandwich so that the jam leaks out of the side. She licks the jam, smacking her lips with exaggerated pleasure.

"Yum," she says. "You sure you don't want one?"

Chinhominey shakes her head, then changes her mind and nods.

"Okay," she says in English, "Okay."

Christina asks, surprised, "Where did you learn that?"

"T.B," Chinhominey says.

Christina makes another foldover peanut butter and jam sandwich. She pours two tall glasses of milk and hands one to her grandmother. The two women chew slowly, standing by the counter, taking loud gulps of milk in between bites. Christina looks up and sees her mother in the doorway.

"Do you want me to cook something? You can't just eat a sandwich. You will be hungry. Lots of food from dinner. *Mandoo* and *bulgogi*," Myung Hee says.

"I'm not hungry. I just had a sandwich."

Her mother looks hurt. Chinhominey makes a smacking sound with her lips.

Myung Hee sits down at the dinner table.

"What happened?" she asks, "You and Henry fight?"

"No, not really. We're just not getting married. I don't really want to talk about it," she says. "There's really nothing to talk about." She pulls her hand away, lifts the glass of milk to her lips, and takes one last long swallow. Myung Hee watches her, wanting to say something, but not knowing what.

Christina rises from the table and carries her empty glass and plate to the sink.

"Really, there's nothing wrong," she says, rinsing her glass and plate. "I'm fine. No problem. Quit worrying. I'm going to bed."

Chinhominey is making moist chewing sounds as she finishes her peanut butter and jam sandwich. Myung Hee turns to her with an annoyed look. "I can't think when you make all those sounds with your mouth!"

Chinhominey swallows and snaps, "Ayew, ayew, look at you. Frustrated because you can't communicate with your own beloved daughter. She won't even tell you why she is unhappy. Why do you have eyes when you can't see? Why do you have ears when you can't hear?"

It is the harsh tone of her voice that forces Myung Hee to remember.

She had been three months pregnant. It was 1970. She, her husband, and their one-year-old daughter, Hyun Choon, were living in her mother-in-law's house a few miles outside of Seoul, as was still the custom in Korean households. One day, Chinhominey burst into her room, without knocking as usual.

"I have bad news," she announced.

"Please," Myung Hee replied, "Don't tell me." Everything her mother-in-law had to say was bad news.

"I visited the Fortune Teller," her mother-in-law continued, as though she were deaf.

"The same one who predicted that my first child would be born with claws!" Myung Hee said, picking up her infant daughter.

Her mother-in-law had been told that if Myung Hee ate crab during her pregnancy, her child would be born with crab claws.

"You were lucky that time," Chinhominey warned. "This time, no more luck. You are not destined to have more than one child. She told me that this next baby will die young!"

"What?"

"This baby will die before its own mother. Her fate is linked with mine!"

"Nonsense!" Myung Hee said. She put Hyun Choon back into the crib.

"You must get rid of the baby."

"Stop! No more!"

"I am only trying to protect you."

Myung Hee started to wail, screaming and crying at the same time. Hyun Choon, hearing her mother, started to howl.

"See! See! It's true! The baby has already possessed you! It is making you crazy!"

"You are making me crazy!" Myung Hee picked up a pillow and started to hit her mother-in-law, swinging at her head in a fury.

Yung Chul, returning from his apprenticeship at Seoul National Bank, heard the commotion and ran into the room. "What is going on? What is happening?"

He rushed toward his wife who still flailed her arms, striking at her mother-in-law.

"Stop it! Stop it!" he yelled at his wife, grabbing her by the wrists and shaking her.

Blinded by tears, she pulled roughly away from her husband, and fled from the house. She ran as fast as she could, her bare feet stumbling over rocks and twigs, running until she couldn't breathe, until she couldn't see, until her legs gave out and she dropped from exhaustion, falling onto the hard gravel road. And that is how she lost her second child.

"So what are you going to do?" Grace asks Christina.

Christina is sitting on her bed, holding the ring in her hands. She looks into space, her eyes fixed on some distant object.

"I don't know," Christina says.

Something in the sisters' relationship has shifted since yesterday; their roles have reversed. Grace feels protective toward her older sister. She realizes that, for once, *she* needs to be careful, she could inadvertently say something that would hurt Christina.

Grace folds her sweater and jeans and stacks them neatly on the floor. Sensing that her sister wants to talk, Grace lingers in the room for a few minutes more, refolds her sweater, adjusts her socks. She is careful not to overstep, but she wants to let her sister know that she is receptive, supportive. "Do you think I should get my hair cut?" Grace finally asks, wanting to continue a dialogue, even though it's not the conversation that either of them wants to have. Christina blinks and looks at her as if for the first time. It has been a long time since Grace has asked Christina for her opinion on anything. It has been a long time since Grace has trusted Christina to respond with kindness.

"Maybe just the ends," she says, "Maybe just a trim."

Grace examines a handful of hair, looking at the ends. She accepts the comment as intended, without putting a malicious spin on it. "Yeah, they are kind of dry," she says.

"So where did you go tonight?" Christina asks.

"To a sushi restaurant."

"With that guy who called last time? What's his name again? Mark?"

"Mike," Grace says almost serenely. She must really like him, Christina thinks. He must be good for her.

"Did he kiss you goodnight?" Christina asks.

"None of your business, nosy," Grace says, but she is smiling with embarrassed pleasure. She rises from the edge of the bed, "I have to brush my teeth." She is about to leave the room when she stops and says, "Yes."

"Was he a good kisser?" Christina asks.

Grace shrugs. "I think so."

Christina smiles and closes her eyes.

Chapter 21

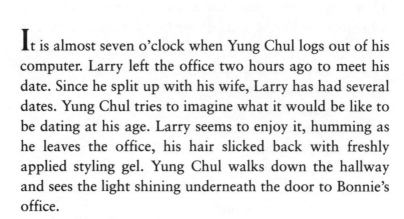

It is almost seven o'clock when Yung Chul logs out of his computer. Larry left the office two hours ago to meet his date. Since he split up with his wife, Larry has had several dates. Yung Chul tries to imagine what it would be like to be dating at his age. Larry seems to enjoy it, humming as he leaves the office, his hair slicked back with freshly applied styling gel. Yung Chul walks down the hallway and sees the light shining underneath the door to Bonnie's office.

"You leaving?" he asks.

"I still have to finish all this," she says, gesturing to the papers spilled across her desk,

"It can wait until tomorrow," he says. "You should go home. The neighborhood's not so safe in the evening."

"In that case," she says, standing up, "I'll walk out with you."

She yawns and stretches. Her dress gapes open at the buttons. Yung Chul catches a glimpse of white lace. He can't help but notice the way Bonnie's dress fits snugly at the waist, across her bottom, ends just above the knee. She has nice legs, he thinks, nice and curvaceous. He reminds himself that she is Christina's age. You could be her father, he thinks. His wife used to have nice legs. It seems like a long time since he last saw them.

They get into the elevator. "You should be careful after dark," he warns, "It's not safe."

You sound like her father, he thinks. She doesn't seem to mind the advice. She doesn't react the way his daughters would. Or his wife. She isn't defensive. She just smiles.

He thinks he hears her say, "You drive me crazy." He looks at her, surprised. She is nonchalantly staring at the floor numbers on the elevator as they light up.

"Excuse me?" he asks.

"I said, the drive is crazy," she says, sighing with exasperation. "It takes me almost an entire hour to get from my apartment to the office."

The elevator stops at the parking level. "You don't have to walk me to my car," she says, "I'll be okay." But Yung Chul walks a couple of steps in front of her, scanning the garage protectively. Bonnie stops in front of a rusty 1979 blue Pontiac.

"Nice car," he says. "Drive carefully. Wear your seatbelt."

Bonnie blinks. She shuts the car door. Yung Chul turns and walks back to where he parked his car. *A wink!* Or was it her contact lenses? No, she winked at him. Could it be that she was flirting? He is old enough to be her father! Not quite. No, not quite. She isn't *that* young. And *he* isn't that old. *Imagine, flirting with him!* He chuckles softly at the thought.

When he pushes the front door open, dread creeps over him. At having to face his own family. His unhappy wife, his unhappy mother, his unhappy children. He remembers when his daughters ran screaming with laughter through the house, chasing each other! The joyful sound of children's laughter.

He smiles, remembering. His daughters were once so playful, so full of life! Calling him Daddy in their little voices, pulling on his pant legs, his shirt, jumping on his lap as though he were a jungle gym, *Appa! Appa!* Making him feel as though he were the most important man in the world when he came home from work, *Appa's home! Appa! Daddy!* Then they came running, they would have knocked him over if they hadn't been so tiny, racing to be the first to be lifted into Daddy's arms, spinning first one, and then the other into the air.

And his wife. Always in the kitchen, walking out to greet him, holding a spoon or a cloth in her hand, her hair pulled back in a scarf, face ruddy from cooking, smelling of sesame oil and ginger, watching as their children jumped all over Daddy. And he looked up and saw her smiling at him — his beautiful wife! — and he wanted to grab her and twirl her around in his arms. The look in his eyes was enough for Myung Hee then, in those days, as he stood, holding a daughter in each arm, the girls pulling at his hair, yanking his ears, tugging at his jacket, telling him stories about what Christina did today, and *Today I saw a frog in the backyard,* and *It wasn't a frog, Daddy, it was a lizard,* and *I want a puppy!*

And then the girls would run off to play, leaving him standing in the hallway alone, facing his wife.

His beautiful wife.

And she would smirk coquettishly and turn her back on him, and return to whatever it was she had been doing in the kitchen tossing her hair as though she had more important things to do than to be with him, so that he vowed to get even with her later, when they were alone, just the two of them, their darling daughters fast asleep and it was just the two of them, and the warmth of her welcoming body. He would make it up to her then, for all the times he had been kept waiting, and she had waited, for all the times they had looked at each other across a room scattered with toys, or across the dinner table, or across the heads of their children, but had to wait, wait until the guests had left, or the children had gone to bed, or the paperwork was finished and he could come home, finally, and be with her, together, just the two of them.

He steps inside the house, pausing, remembering the way it used to be. Nobody comes to greet him. Nobody seems to care.

Once again, he lies awake, staring at the ceiling. Myung Hee is curled away from him, on her side, hands are clasped against the side of her face as if in prayer. What does she think when she is pretending to be asleep? Is she still worrying about the children? The way she used to so many years ago when she awoke at the slightest sound, afraid that one of them might have awakened from a bad dream.

Back then, he would have sat up next to her. He always awoke when she did, as if they shared the same dreams, as if they shared even that. He would reassure her that it was nothing, it was just the wind, it was the dog barking next door, or a car driving by outside their window. He would hold her, stroke her hair, feel her warm body press against his until it warmed him up, too. He would hold her in his arms until she closed her eyes, like a child, until she fell asleep in his arms, and he held her, not wanting to let go, leaning her against pillows, his arms still wrapped around her, holding her close against him, not letting go, he would never let her go, listening as her breathing evened out, restful, peaceful, not the way it is now when she pretends to be asleep.

Chapter 22

It is almost six o'clock. Yung Chul glances again at his watch. Bonnie hasn't left yet. Only three more minutes. Three minutes more. Then he will march down the hall, knock on her door, wait for her to tell him to come in.

She will look at him, smiling flirtatiously. She will be flirting with him, more boldly tonight, he is sure of it. She will let whatever happens, happen. And he is tired of waiting. He will speed up the process. He is tired of letting others decide for him. He has made up his mind. He is going to offer to walk her to her car and then, when they are in the elevator, alone, he will ask her, nonchalantly, "Let's get a drink, there's no rush getting home."

He will say this calmly, acting very cool, as if he did this all the time, as if he didn't mean anything by it. He already knows where they will go. A bar, the Orion, just down the street. He has been to the bar a few times with Larry. It is a nice bar, jazz playing in the background, not too loud, soft lighting. A young crowd. Bonnie will feel comfortable. They will order a couple of drinks, sit in one of the small booths in the back, and just talk. The drinks will help them relax, loosen their tongues.

And afterwards? He hasn't thought about that yet. Well, not much. It will just be a couple of drinks; he isn't going to get all worked up over nothing. He doesn't want to deal with the questions, the practical questions, Where would they go afterwards? How would he suggest it?

He realizes he is already feeling a little guilty. Even though nothing has happened. Yet. Probably. But his palms are sweating and his heart is beating a rhythm in his brain, giving him a slight headache, pressing down on his eyelids.

He has never cheated on his wife. Not in twenty-five years of marriage.

But you have to live, he tells himself, You have to live. You can't live your life in a state of numbness. You're not living, you're existing, you're stuck. Your wheels spinning in the mud.

You're stuck. Stuck.

I'm living in fear, he thinks. Fear of moving forward, fear of moving on.

He puts on his new Italian jacket that his wife bought for him, and walks out the door with firm steps. He sees the light shining through the crack underneath the door. He glances at his watch. Six o'clock. It is time. Time to move on. He raises his hand to knock on her door, when the phone in his office rings. He hesitates and then turns back down the hallway.

"Hey, I'm glad you're still there."

It's Larry.

"Do you think you could meet me? Have a few beers?"

"Is anything wrong?"

"Yeah," Larry says. His voice wavers slightly and then he says, "The divorce became final today. I'm down the street. At the Orion, you know the one."

"Sure. I know it." Yung Chul says wryly.

He replaces the receiver. He walks out the door again, this time with less spring in his step, more resignation than determination in the set of his jaw. He stops outside Bonnie's office, knocks once, opens the door. She is sitting behind her desk. Her hair is brushed, and her lips are shiny with freshly applied lip gloss.

"I wanted to say goodnight."

"Oh," she says, looking with surprise at her clock, "Is it seven already?"

"Young lady," he says with mock disappointment, "I thought I told you not to stay past five o'clock."

"Are you walking down to the parking garage?" she asks. "I'll walk down with you."

"No, I'm going to meet Larry," he says, "He's at the bar down the street. His divorce became final today. I think he wants to talk."

"Oh," she says, "I think I'll stay a little while longer. I want to finish some work. Anyway, there's no big hurry to get home."

As Yung Chul walks to the elevator, he thinks, There are so many people in the world. And yet, everyone seems so alone.

Larry is sitting at the bar, shoulders slumped. He is wearing a black and white checkered sports jacket, and his hair is slicked back with pomade.

Yung Chul sits on the stool next to him. "I see you started without me," he remarks.

Larry lifts his tumbler to his lips and drains it. "Yeah, well, I've had a shitty day. Real shitty."

He motions the bartender for another drink.

"How long have you been here?" Yung Chul asks.

"Not too long. Maybe four hours," Larry replies.

"Four hours?"

"Since about two o'clock. When the divorce became final. We just signed the papers. Just like that," he says, snapping his fingers. "Just like that and it's all over." For several months, Larry has talked about nothing else but how much he wished the whole ordeal of the divorce would be over, finished. Then he could start a new life.

"Yeah, yeah, yeah," Larry says bitterly. He shakes his head, "Don't ever get a divorce."

"You're the one who wanted it," Yung Chul reminds him. "You were the one who didn't like feeling tied down." He sounds harsher than he intends to, the reprimand directed at himself as much as it is at Larry.

"Yeah, I was the one," Larry admits. "I was the one. I was the one who wanted to fool around. I was the one who wanted to stay out and party."

He stares into space, his eyes filling with tears.

"She was there," he says, after a long silence. "I finally saw her."

He looks down for a minute, and now he is crying. Yung Chul pats his friend on the shoulder.

"She looked great," Larry whispers. "Fantastic."

"You could always change your mind. You're the one who wanted it, remember?"

Larry shakes his head. "It's too late. There's no turning back."

"She found another man?"

"No. But she seemed . . . different. I don't think she loves me anymore," Larry says. He looks bewildered. "It's different to be married to someone. You see them everyday,

164

in the morning when they don't look so good. They're kind of crabby before coffee. You hear them when they go to the bathroom, stuff like that. After a while, there's no mystery left, you know? But I loved her. I still love her. When I saw her today, she took my breath away. If I saw her in a bar, I wouldn't even try to talk to her, she'd be out of my league. But when we were married, every woman I met was more attractive, more exciting. Now I can't even go out with the same woman for more than a week. They all drive me crazy."

He starts crying again, shaking his head miserably. "Funny thing is, it's those little things that I miss the most. Like the way she made this gurgling noise when she brushed her teeth — it used to drive me nuts! Or the way she left her shoes by the bed so I was always tripping over them. Those were the things that sometimes bugged me, but now, I miss them the most. It was stuff like that, made it a marriage. Now that I don't have Rose anymore, I realize that I didn't want her out of my life. I just didn't want to be married."

The words hit Yung Chul unexpectedly. He drinks his beer in silence. Hadn't he already taken the first step in his mind? It starts like that, he thinks. In the heart and in the mind, even before the first kiss. He had already betrayed his wife in his heart. In his daydreams, he was willing to throw away twenty-five years of marriage, for what?

Larry shakes his head in disbelief and drains his single malt. His hands tremble as he returns the glass to the counter.

"You want to come over for dinner?" Yung Chul says. "You shouldn't stay here and drink alone." Regret rushes through his body as he thinks about his wife. Beautiful Myung Hee, who has always been there for him, raising their children, making a home for them. How could he have been willing to let her go? What would have happened if Larry had not called? If Chance had not intervened?

"No. I think I'll go home. Maybe rent a movie."

As Yung Chul starts to leave, he looks at Larry again, one hand underneath his chin, slumped forward.

"You're coming to my house for dinner," he insists.

"I'm okay," Larry says, "I just can't believe how stupid I was." He finishes the rest of his drink and stands up, wavering unsteadily on his feet.

"Leave your car here overnight. I'll give you a lift home."

"I'm okay . . ."

"You're a stupid guy, remember?" Yung Chul says, "Don't argue with me."

As they walk out of the bar, Yung Chul feels strangely free.

The table is set for one when he gets home. He walks upstairs, toward the bedroom, where Myung Hee is sitting in front of the dressing table, in her bathrobe, applying cold cream to her face. She doesn't turn when he walks into the room.

"I'm sorry I'm late," he says. He closes the door behind him. Myung Hee continues applying the cold cream.

"Have you been drinking?" she asks, looking at his face in the mirror.

"One beer," he says. "I'm not drunk."

She wipes at her face with a tissue. He touches her hair lightly, but she doesn't look up.

"You have so many gray hairs," he whispers. He sounds as though he is somehow responsible.

166

"Of course," she says. "You don't remember all the times I sat here and tried to pluck them out."

He strokes her hair, gently, then presses his face against the back of her neck, nuzzling her neck. She freezes, immobilized. He touches her hair, her cheek, kisses the nape of her neck.

"I don't know why I stopped looking," he says.

He takes Myung Hee's hands and gently, turns her toward him. She stares at him, as though at a stranger.

He kisses her, on the forehead, on her cheeks, on her eyelids, tasting the sweetness of her cold cream, feeling the texture of her skin, feeling her facial muscles tense and then soften, relax, the lines smooth out. He strokes her neck, the lump in her throat, tracing her collarbone with his fingertips, looking at her in wonder, She is beautiful! Still so beautiful. She is watching him, wary, uncertain. He touches her feet, feeling the hardness of her heel, the smoothness of the arch, lightly, until she can no longer watch, until her eyes flutter shut. Then he pulls at the sash on her robe and it falls open. He leans back on his heels, watching her, her robe open, sitting still. Her back straight. Sitting very still.

He takes each of her hands in his and then they are standing, facing each other, his eyes searching, intense. She looks away, unable to stand the intensity of his gaze. He pulls her toward him, close, against him, until he can feel her heart beating against his chest. He holds her tightly, moving to the rhythm of her heartbeat, his heartbeat, his shirt damp with perspiration, with anticipation, as he moves her, moves with her, gently, swaying, dancing cheek-to-cheek, the way they used to, remembering the way it used to be. He leads her over to the bed, lies down with her.

"The children," she whispers. "What if they come in?"

167

He kisses her lips, to stop her from worrying, stop her worries. He moves down, strokes her ankles, and her calves, and the impossibly smooth spot behind her knee, he kisses her there, where the skin is warm and moist, running his fingertips up her leg, the inside of her thigh, softer, measured breaths, careful breaths, still careful, until she stops breathing, holds her breath. Waiting.

He continues stroking the inside of her thigh, the softness of her skin hypnotizing him, as he kisses her, her flesh warm, hot, making him dizzy, making his blood rush. And her breathing, he can hear her breathing now. She is no longer holding her breath.

His heart expands with love for his wife, filling up his chest with a kind of sorrow, sweet sorrow, until there is no room left for anything else, no room for pain now, or regrets, no room, even, for pride, only space enough for her, to let her in. Myung Hee closes her eyes, reaches for her husband, touches him, wanting him, too, as they move to a different rhythm, their bodies in tune to the music, in a different kind of dance.

Chapter 23

It is only natural for a mother to want the best for her son. But that was not the only reason that I felt compelled to protect Yung Chul. I am his mother, but I am not a martyr. It was a promise I had made to my husband. A promise that I hoped would undo my betrayal.

After the end of our first year of marriage, I had still not conceived so I returned to the Fortune Teller's house. The front door was open. She was drinking tea, her hunched back turned to me.

"Come in," she said, without turning around. "Come in and sit down. I will tell you where you can find him."

"Who?" I asked.

"The man who will father your child," she answered. She took a long sip of tea, making a slurping sound with her lips.

We walked through the woods behind the Fortune Teller's shack. We walked to a part of the woods that I had never been to. The Fortune Teller led me to a tree with branches that hung to the ground. She pulled aside one of the branches and motioned for me to step inside. It took a moment for my eyes to adjust to the darkness. Then I saw the man standing in front of me.

The man she chose to father my child was very short and not at all handsome. I am surprised that my son turned out to be tall and good-looking. He must have inherited most of my genes. The man was very quiet. I never learned his name, but I can never forget his face. There are so many things that I can no longer remember, my mind fails me. But that afternoon remains with me. I remember everything — the dampness of the dirt, the suffocating smell of rotting leaves, the man's broad flat face, the pungent metallic smell rising from his arm pits, the heavy press of his fat belly against my flat one, his flaring nostrils, the cold clammy feel of his rough hands. Even now, so many years later, remembering makes me hurt.

During the eighth month of my pregnancy, I had strange dreams. I dreamt of fire-breathing dragons with lashing tongues and tails the size of entire villages. The dreams caused me to wake up in the middle of the night, my heart pounding so loud that it disturbed my husband's sleep.

When I described the dreams to my mother-in-law, she smiled.

"That means you will give birth to a boy," she said, putting one hand over mine. She looked happy. It was the first time that I had ever been able to make my mother-in-law happy.

It wasn't until many years later that I learned that the father of my son was the husband of the old woman who had told my fortune.

"But he's so much younger than you!" I exclaimed.

"Yes," she said, with a satisfied smile, "But there are some things that are more important than age."

"But why? Why would anyone, why would a woman . . . ?" I couldn't finish the question.

"Why would a woman want her husband to father another woman's child?" she asked.

I nodded.

"Because she wants him to live forever," she answered, "And I was too old to do that for him."

My husband was a very good man. A good father and a good husband. He never said anything when he saw that his son's eyes were smaller than his own, or that his hair was thick and wavy while my husband's was fine and straight. His son grew up and became a kind, intelligent man, like my husband, his father in name if not in blood. If my husband suspected anything, he never let me know. He treated my son as if he were his own.

When Yung Chul cried in the middle of the night, it was my husband who awakened. He would kiss me on the cheek and tell me to continue dreaming. Then he would carry our son in his arms until the crying stopped.

You see how my husband cared about me? Even after we were married. Most husbands stop trying to please their wives the day after the wedding ceremony. But not my husband. He brought to me sweet rice cakes for no reason. He prepared for me tea. He held my hand in his simply because we were walking through the streets. Our love would have lasted forever — it is the one thing of which I am certain — if fate had not intervened.

It happened early one morning. It was a neighbor who told us. He ran into our house without knocking. I was still in my pajamas. I remember clearly his face. It was red, and drops of sweat were rolling down his cheeks like teardrops. I remember the look in his eyes, like a scared mountain rabbit. I remember everything about the way he looked, but I do not remember his name.

"Quickly!" he shouted. "You must leave quickly." He turned toward my husband, "As soon as possible!"

"What has happened?" my husband asked. He was much calmer than this neighbor whose name I have forgotten.

"The Communists have invaded the country!" he cried, "In the middle of the night!"

"What need is there to worry?" I asked. "The Americans will protect us."

My neighbor shook his head, so vigorously that I thought it might fall off.

"No! No! No! Even the Americans have been taken by surprise. They have captured American soldiers! They are dragging people out of their beds! They are killing the rich!"

He grabbed my husband by the shoulders.

"You must go," he pleaded. "They will kill you if they find you. You are wealthy. You are educated. You will be the first to die!"

I tried to stay calm. Perhaps my neighbor was exaggerating. But then I saw the look in my husband's eyes. His were the eyes of a tiger that I had once seen as a little girl, a white tiger, that was captured in the mountains when I was growing up.

"You take our son," he said. "And go to live with Sang Bok."

Sang Bok was a poor cousin of my husband's. He lived

in Pulguksan, a small village a few miles east. My husband knew that the North Koreans had no interest in the uneducated peasants. They would think I was Sang Bok's simple wife.

"And what about you?"

"I will go west," he said. "The soldiers will be heading south, to capture the country. You must go. All will be well," my husband said, holding me for the last time. "You will see. But you must make sure that nothing happens to our son. You must protect him. He is the future."

He kissed me on the mouth and then he was gone, forever.

So you see? I could not forsake my parental obligation even if I had wanted to. I had made a promise to my husband to protect my son, our son. Yung Chul may have carried the blood of another man, but he carried the soul of my husband. His quiet courage, his curious intellect, his kind and gentle manner — all were learned from my husband. My son was the future and without him, my husband's memory would die with me. I had to protect my son, even if, in so doing, I turned him against me.

Chapter 24

In a dress and pearls instead of her usual faded housedress, Mrs. Choi places the steaming casserole pot on the table next to the platter of bulgogi.

"Why are you so dressed up?" Christina asks, "You're wearing pearls and a silk dress."

"Not silk. Polyester," Myung Hee says taking a seat.

Yung Chul looks at his wife, his eyes bright and shining. Chinhominey watches her son and her daughter-in-law carefully.

"What is that smell?" she asks, sniffing the air.

"Kimchee chige," Myung Hee replies, "Bulgogi."

"No, not that," Chinhominey says, shaking her head. "The other smell. Smells like old water in a vase of dead flowers."

"I don't smell anything," Yung Chul says, sniffing the air, "Nothing but kimchee chige and bulgogi, and sweet perfume."

He smiles at his wife who blushes.

"Aha! Perfume. You're wearing perfume," Chinhominey says in an accusatory tone, turning to her daughter-in-law. "It makes me sneeze." She gasps, as if she were about to sneeze, but doesn't.

"Caroline's mother called me today. She told me that Caroline got accepted to Stanford law school," Myung Hee says, changing the subject. Grace stops chewing. "You should hear soon," Myung Hee adds.

"Well, it depends. Some people hear months before other people. It depends on when you sent your application," Grace says.

"In the next few days," Myung Hee says. "She told me that Caroline also heard from Harvard, but she was rejected. She pretends that she prefers to go to Stanford anyway. I told her that you prefer to go to Harvard. I told her that Harvard is your number one choice." Both parents are beaming proudly at their daughter.

"I don't even know if I want to go to law school, remember? I might want to do something else."

Yung Chul shakes his head, "Of course you will go to Harvard. First Choi to go to Harvard." He looks so happy that Grace feels like leaping up with a rebel yell and overturning the dinner table, wants to hear the plates crash to the floor, wants to see the astonished look on her parents' faces. They don't care about me, Grace fumes, her heart pounding. They only care about themselves, how to look good in front of their friends.

She stares at her plate of bulgogi. She feels a cramp develop in her stomach, anxiety flexing its muscle. Her head start to throb. I have to get out of here, she thinks, all the voices are stealing her oxygen, she can't breathe. *You don't belong here. You have no place here.*

Chinhominey sneezes so violently that the table shakes and water splashes out of the glasses. "Your perfume makes me sneeze. Smells like dead flowers. Terrible smell," Chinhominey says, holding her hand to her nose, "Terrible."

They didn't call me when Grace was born, but I knew anyway. One morning, I felt a sharp pain in my stomach. The pain was so sharp that I fell to my knees right in the middle of the street! A man rushed to assist me, but I pushed him away. It was my daughter-in-law who was truly in pain on the other side of the Pacific Ocean. Somewhere in America my second granddaughter was being born.

All day long I waited for the phone call. I waited so long that it became night, and then it became day again. Still no telephone call from my only son telling me that my second granddaughter had been born.

I quickly walked to the Fortune Teller's house to learn what she knew. I walked so quickly that by the time she opened the door, I was out of breath.

"Tell me what happened!" I demanded.

"I was going to say to you the same," she replied.

I removed my shoes and put on the slippers that she had placed by the door. I entered her house without waiting for her to ask me. See how familiar with her I had become!

"Yesterday, my granddaughter was born," I said. "But now I am afraid that something has happened to her."

"Nothing has happened to your granddaughter," she said, placing a cup of tea in front of me.

My hands were shaking. I picked up the teacup with both hands.

"How do you know?"

"Because you are here," she said. "Have you lost your memory? Have you forgotten your fortune?"

I took a sip of tea and burned my tongue.

"As long as *you* live, your granddaughter will live. Her fate is tied to yours."

I blew on my tea.

"Your good fortune is *her* good fortune. Your misfortune is *her* misfortune."

The Fortune Teller chanted this and then closed her eyes.

"What can I do?"

"There is nothing you can do," she said. "Fate has already decided."

"Tell me what I must do to change fate!" I said, throwing all my money onto the table.

The old woman laughed, showing black spaces in her mouth where there were once teeth.

"It's not so easy," she said. "I cannot tell you."

I started to pick up the money I had thrown onto the table. The old woman pushed away my hand.

"I cannot tell you today," she said, "but maybe tomorrow, something will change."

I loved my second granddaughter even before I had met her. That is why I knew the Fortune Teller's words to be true. My fate *was* linked to hers! Otherwise I would not have thought about her from the moment I woke up in the morning to the moment I fell asleep at night.

Before my second granddaughter was born, I ate and drank whatever I pleased. But after her birth, I took care of my health. I stopped drinking coffee and started to drink ginseng. How I hated the bitter taste of ginseng. Even with a tablespoon of honey, it tasted like old medicine! But for the sake of my granddaughter, I drank a large cup every morning to give me energy. I went for a long walk every evening to improve my heart. I started to read lots of books to improve my mind.

Several weeks after my granddaughter was born, the telephone rang. It was my son. I knew it was him even before he spoke.

"Uhmahnee," he said.

"Is she healthy?" I asked immediately.

"She is so healthy that my poor wife never sleeps."

"You help your wife. She already has one daughter to take care of," I said. "Be careful with your daughter."

"We have two daughters."

"There is only one we need to worry about," I reminded him. "Don't pretend you have forgotten. Your second daughter is the one you were not supposed to have."

"Good-bye. Take care of your health."

"I am taking very good care of my health," I reassured him.

Chapter 25

Twigs. Crackers. Cereal. Fingers. Things that snap.

The children are restless. They tap their fingers, shuffle their feet, whisper to each other, as Christina reads aloud to them about a president named Abraham Lincoln who was tall and smart and born in a log cabin.

"He was very poor," she says, "but he wanted to help others who were even worse off than he was."

The second graders don't care. They continue to fidget, doodling on the desks with their pencils, playing with their erasers, not listening to the teacher. Out of the corner of her eye, Christina can see Luis throwing paper balls at Alexander, occasionally hitting him. Alexander tries to ignore him. Luis throws an eraser. Alexander picks up the eraser and throws it back at Luis. Christina looks up. Immediately, Alexander and Luis face the front of the classroom, hands folded on their desks.

"Luis, what are you doing?"

"Nothing, ma'am." Luis' face is red. He likes Miss Choi. All the kids like Miss Choi. She is nice. She is pretty. She never gets mad.

"But you're supposed to be listening," she says. "You're not supposed to be doing nothing, are you?"

"I am listening, Miss Choi," Luis says. He wants her to like him. All the kids want Miss Choi to like them.

"If you're listening, then why are you throwing things at Alexander?"

Luis shrugs, "I wasn't."

Christina throws down her book. It slams against the floor. The second graders wince. She walks over to Luis, who is still staring straight ahead, his face hot, afraid to look at Miss Choi. She crouches down and grabs him by the shoulders. He is accustomed to the wrath of adults. She shakes him. His head wiggles back and forth.

"Don't lie to me," she warns. "Don't ever lie to me!"

He starts to cry. She lets him go. She straightens up, feels twenty-five pairs of eyes on her back. Fifty eyes full of surprise and fear. They are afraid of her now.

The images reappear. Twigs, Crackers, Cereal, Fingers. She picks up her book and tries to find the place where she left off, but her hands are trembling, making it hard to turn the pages. She sits down in her chair, book in her lap, and continues reading. The children are quiet, afraid to move, listening in fearful silence as she reads aloud, her voice quivering slightly as she reminds them of the importance of working hard and being honest.

Chapter 26

Somewhere in the distance, a clock strikes twelve. Midnight.

You almost hit that kid. You came that close to hitting him. That close!

Christina climbs out of the bed and makes her way down the hallway, careful not to make noise, to the bathroom. She shuts the door behind her and turns on the light. Face to face with her own reflection. She doesn't look so beautiful now. Not at this hour, not at this moment. Her eyes are tired and red, her skin is sallow, blemishes mar her usually smooth complexion. Her lips are chapped and peeling. The facade is crumbling.

She opens the cabinet underneath the sink and takes out her cosmetic kit. She shakes a bottle of foundation, opens it, pours a little onto her finger. She smoothes it over her face, covering the blemishes, the fine lines, the bumps, until it looks smooth and clear. She looks for eyeliner, black liquid eyeliner. She lines the top and bottom of one eye, then the other. Broad strokes, thick strokes. Not a natural look, not tonight. Tonight, she wants to be made-up. Tonight she doesn't want to look like herself. Anything but. Anyone but. Eyeshadow. Deep purple eyeshadow, silver frost on the brow bone. Blusher. More eyeliner. Lipliner to make her lips fuller, then lipstick. Bright red. Scarlet red. She examines her face.

You look like a whore, she thinks. Like a whore.

She applies more lipstick. Mascara on the upper lashes, then on the lower lashes. Like a painted lady. More lipstick. More blush. More mascara. Black clumps cling to her eyelashes. Little black dots stain her eyelids. She picks up a hairbrush and starts to tease her hair, working from the ends to the roots. She spritzes hairspray, short pumps, making her hair sticky, hard and spikey. She brushes backwards, until her hair sticks up, brushing harder, tearing at her hair, making it a rat's nest, so that it doesn't lie flat and smooth, so that it looks brittle and unkempt and unwashed.

She tiptoes back to her bedroom, around Grace, who is sleeping on the floor. Without turning on the light, Christina pulls a dress out of her closet. A short black dress, one that she has never worn, that she bought on a lark one day when she went shopping on Melrose Avenue. She wiggles into the dress, pulling it down over her hips. It clings to her and ends just below the crotch. She fumbles at the bottom of her closet for a pair of shoes. Black spike heels, she has worn them only once. Three inch spike heels. On sale. She bought them only because they were so cheap.

In her car, she starts the engine and drives off, without turning on the headlights. In the window, peering at her from between the curtains, Chinhominey is standing. She waves at Christina before the curtains fall back into place.

Although it is a Wednesday night, a line of people wait to get into the club. Christina sets her mouth into a sneer, tosses her tangled mane. She can feel eyes on her, checking her out, her face, her hair, her legs. She is an amalgamation of body parts. She puts her hands on her hips, a defensive gesture. When the line moves, she struts forward, refusing to be cowed by curious stares, interested looks. The bouncer gives her the up and down, looks her directly in the eyes. She stares back for once, doesn't look away.

"Just walk straight in," he tells her, letting her know that she doesn't have to pay. A fringe benefit of being an attractive woman, alone. Something to offset having to endure crude remarks, whistles, mutterings, unwanted stares: Hey baby, looking good, Smile, sweetheart, let's see you smile, Mmmm, nice. . . Christina makes her way across the crowded room, swinging her hips, one leg in front of the other, running her fingers through her hair.

The music is loud, rapid, techno beat, swirling lights. The crowd is young, mostly male, touching her as she walks by, placing a hand on her waist, on her ass, her back, guiding her through the crowd, Beautiful, you're lookin' good tonight, sweetheart, she walks around the club, wandering, pretending to look for something, someone. Then she leans against a wall. She doesn't have long to wait. A man approaches her.

"Hey, what happened? Your man leave you?"

She shakes her head, doesn't smile, stares straight ahead, bored.

"You feel like dancing? You want to dance with me?"

"No," she says, not rudely, but not apologetically either.

"That's cool, that's cool. I can handle that," he says, backing away. "You need anything I'll be right over there."

The music is too loud, the lights are too bright, the room is too dark. She feels herself sway. She grabs onto a post, standing there, her head spinning, faster and faster, then slower, like being on a carousel when she was a kid, her parents waving to her, holding a camera, smile pretty for the camera, waving back, waving although she felt sick, although she wanted to get off, the horses were slowing down, slowing, then stopped, but she felt like she was still spinning, even when she was on solid ground, even when she was walking, when her legs were moving, the earth seemed to continue, spinning around, she couldn't stop it, going around and around until she thought she would fall, until she thought she would fall spinning into the ground, like a drill, deep into the earth.

"You okay?"

She looks up. A man is looking at her, his forehead furrowed, concerned.

She nods. Yes, I'm fine, she wants to say, I'm fine. Nothing's wrong. Everything is fine. She opens her mouth but nothing comes out. He reaches out, grabs her, catches her.

"Are you sick? What's the matter? What are you on?"

Suddenly she starts to cry. People stare as they walk by, puzzled looks. Rubberneckers, wanting to see the crash and burn of somebody else's life. She is crying, harder, against his neck, this complete stranger, she doesn't know who he is, she doesn't even know his name.

"Do you need to see a doctor? Did someone hurt you?" he asks, his voice soft, embarrassed, wanting to help. The lights swirl about her, confusing her, the music in the club is so loud that she can barely hear the words that she tells this stranger, words that she has been unable to speak to anyone, even to herself.

"I'm pregnant."

Chapter 27

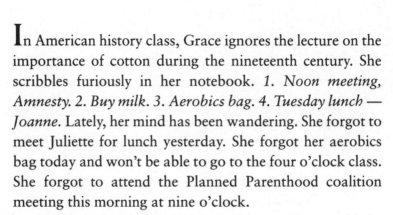

In American history class, Grace ignores the lecture on the importance of cotton during the nineteenth century. She scribbles furiously in her notebook. *1. Noon meeting, Amnesty. 2. Buy milk. 3. Aerobics bag. 4. Tuesday lunch — Joanne.* Lately, her mind has been wandering. She forgot to meet Juliette for lunch yesterday. She forgot her aerobics bag today and won't be able to go to the four o'clock class. She forgot to attend the Planned Parenthood coalition meeting this morning at nine o'clock.

But she didn't forget the history lecture. How could she forget? This is the only class she has with Mike. Although she did spend too long getting dressed this morning and walked into the lecture fifteen minutes late. She is wearing jeans and a peach colored blouse, one of Christina's hand-me-downs. She has even put on a touch of lipstick and a coat of mascara.

"If I didn't know any better," Frances whispers, "I'd think you were in love."

"Yeah, right," Grace says, with a giggle.

Maybe I *am* in love. She glances over her shoulder. Mike

is sitting at the back of the room staring off into space, his chin resting on his hand, his eyes glazed over, a smile flirting at the corners of his mouth. He looks the way I feel, she thinks. He feels the same way.

Mike is waiting for her outside the lecture hall.

"You were fifteen minutes late to class," he says. She blushes. He noticed! She doesn't tell him that the reason she was late was because she was getting dressed for him.

"Can I walk with you?" he asks. They walk down the hill toward the commons. Mike suddenly stops.

"Can we talk?" he asks. They sit down on a bench, a gift courtesy of the Class of 1928. His Adam's apple moves up and down as he swallows. "Last night, Elizabeth came over. She felt really bad. You know, about everything."

Grace's internal organs come to a screeching halt.

"So . . . anyway, we decided to maybe, you know, like try to work things out. You know, kind of see what happens. So . . . anyway, I just thought that you might want to know that, or that you should know that. Even though, you probably don't really care that much. I mean, it's not like we were going out or anything like that, although I think you're really nice, and I like you a lot."

"Yeah." Grace stares carefully ahead. Is her heart still pumping?

"So, it's cool, isn't it? I mean, everything. I mean, what I said, that's okay, isn't it?"

"Yeah, sure. Of course it's okay."

He smiles, relieved. "Good," he says, "Because, I don't know, I felt kind of funny about it. I mean, I know that you probably felt like the whole thing was no big deal, but still,

187

I didn't want things to be weird between us because I did really like you a lot and I had a lot of fun with you. I mean, I *do* like you a lot."

Grace thinks she feels a faint pulse. *Get it over with.*

"Although in six months, you'd probably have gotten sick of me, and the whole issue would have been mute."

"Moot."

"Yeah. Right. Moot," he says, "But now we can still be friends. That is, if you want."

Grace nods. Don't think about it just yet, she tells herself, as her brain sends a message to her legs to get up. Don't think; just breathe. Wait until you are out of his line of vision.

She walks across campus, toward the parking lot. The throbbing in her head increases its tempo, pressing down on her left eyelid. She wants to go to bed. The sun is shining, but dark clouds are moving quickly across the sky. By the time she reaches her car, raindrops have started to fall. She clears her throat. It does feel kind of scratchy. Maybe I can stay in bed for a few days. Maybe a month. Maybe I have an incurable disease. Maybe I can die tomorrow. Or will it be a long gruesome ending? She imagines herself coughing up blood in a hospital bed, her white gown splattered with red, her hair falling out in clumps, lesions on her face and neck. She can almost hear herself hacking and wheezing out the last bit of life while the nurses impatiently wait outside the room for her to die. Another patient needs her bed.

She parks her car at the curb outside her house. At the

mailbox, she pulls out an envelope with her name on it. From Harvard law school. She rips it open.

Dear Applicant:
We regret to inform you that your application for admission has been rejected . . .

We don't want you. You're not good enough for us.
She crumples up the letter, sticks it into her jacket pocket. She turns and gets back into her car, revs up the engine, presses down on the accelerator, driving further and further away from that place called home.

Chapter 28

It is like a disease, an affliction. Her tongue that she cannot control. The lips that move before she can stop them, before she knows what she is about to say.

The words that bring unhappiness. So much unhappiness. The sadness in her son's eyes. The look on his wife's face. The way her two grandchildren stare at her, with irritation, with hatred!

What's the point in wearing perfume at the dinner table? We are going no place fancy. He was looking at her the way he used to, like an obedient puppy. Even though their marriage cannot last. But he looked so happy when they first sat down to dinner. They could be so happy. Could be. The pain returns. It emanates from her center and spreads to her chest, between her shoulder blades, between her temples, reaches down to her toes. Chinhominey clutches her stomach as pain shoots out of every muscle, every joint, of her body. Prophecies become self-fulfilling. Expectations shape behavior. Fate becomes future. *As long as you are alive, they will be unhappy.* She rolls herself into a small ball at the foot of the bed and closes her eyes. The pain intensifies, like a flame burning brighter, hotter, before flickering out.

There is a small group of protesters in front of the clinic, standing lazily, holding signs.

A minor procedure, Christina tells herself, You'll be out in a couple of hours.

She had told her mother she was going to a Teachers' Association meeting and wouldn't be home for dinner.

She pulls into the outpatient parking lot and turns off the engine. Her hands are shaking.

You have no other choice, she reminds herself. What else are you supposed to do?

You can't tell Amma and Appa. You can't. You have no choice. She leans her head on the steering wheel. I don't want it. I don't want this decision. She opens the car door. There is no fuckin' decision. There is no alternative. You can't do this on your own. You can't bring a child up by yourself. You can't.

And it would break their hearts. Amma and Appa. To know that you had screwed up. Their darling, favorite daughter. Unmarried, pregnant. A disgrace to her family. It's a no-win situation. Heads you win, tails I lose. There is no you. Just me. Just me. What do I want to do? It doesn't matter what I want. It doesn't matter at all.

She takes a seat on a hard orange chair. On the other side of the room, a girl, no more than fifteen or sixteen, taps her feet nervously against the floor. She is pale, her hair straggly, unwashed. The girl, feeling Christina's gaze, turns her head. Christina looks away, feeling guilty. Where is your mom? Where is your dad? Do they know where you are? Did you tell them?

The girl plays with a lock of hair, twirling it around her finger.

Where is your boyfriend? You know who I'm talking about. The boy who did this to you. What promises did he make? Did he tell you that he would never leave you? Did he tell you that? What other lies did he tell you? Are you doing this to keep him? Is he making you do this? She turns back to the girl who is picking at her cuticles, willing the little girl to look at her, Don't be afraid. Don't be afraid. Don't you know? You don't have to do anything that you don't want to do. Don't you know? It's your decision. What do you want to do? The girl frowns slightly, puts her hand to her mouth, starts to gnaw at her fingernails. Don't do that, Christina wants to tell her, Don't bite your fingernails.

"Choi?"

Christina looks up. The nurse is standing in front of her with a kind smile. "Are you Christina Choi?"

Traffic is slow on the streets, so Grace decides to take the freeway. The rain has washed away the smog. The sky is bright and clear. The buildings look taller, their edges sharper. The palm trees toss their freshly shampooed fronds in the light breeze, and the sun scatters the few remaining clouds across the sky. A beautiful day. Grace rolls down the window, letting the cool air whip her hair around her head. She continues driving, chasing the sunshine. The Pacific Ocean laps against the coastline, slapping the rocks, receding into itself, advance and retreat, a continuous dance between earth and sea. If Grace glances over her shoulder, she can see it. But she doesn't. She looks straight ahead,

192

presses her foot to the accelerator. The speedometer spins to sixty-five, seventy, seventy-five. Reckless, irresponsible. The engine rumbles angrily. She shifts in her seat. She stopped only once, someplace just north of Santa Barbara, to fill up on gas. Her stomach rumbles. She reaches for the bag of chips on the passenger seat beside her. A few crumbs left in the bottom. She pours them into the palm of her hand, licks them up with her tongue. She rolls down the window and screams. A cry of freedom. It doesn't matter anymore, she doesn't have to try anymore. She passes the sign on her left. San Francisco. Seventy-five miles. She smiles. Here I come. She presses on the accelerator. Seventy-seven, seventy-nine, eighty, eighty-five, and not a cop in sight.

Yung Chul pulls into the garage, late for dinner. After work, he went with Larry to have a couple of drinks at the Orion. Bonnie had called in sick.

The house is dark and silent. No food on the table. Nothing. Puzzled, he walks into the kitchen, switches on the light. There is a note next to the telephone, in his wife's handwriting. He picks it up, clutches it in his hand. His heart sinks into his stomach.

The telephone rings, shrill, jarring him out of his thoughts. He stares at it, hostile. It rings once, twice, three times. He picks it up.

"Hello?"

"Darling?"

It is Myung Hee. He feels weak.

"Did you get my note?"

He quickly reads the note, *Your mother wasn't feeling well. I took her to St. Matthew's Hospital.*

193

"She says she has a stomachache. But they can't find anything wrong. She wants you to come and get her. Your duty, she says, as her only son." Myung Hee hesitates, "Is Grace home yet?"

He understands her concern, hears the edge in her voice.

"No," Yung Chul says, "Nobody is home. But don't worry. I'll be at the hospital in twenty minutes."

He hangs up the phone, closes his eyes in silent prayer. He knows now why his mother has come to visit and why she has stayed so long. She did not want to die alone.

All hospitals look the same, Yung Chul thinks as he walks down the hall. Long narrow corridors, doctors and nurses in white and green smocks, visitors with grim faces, everyone looks so sad, so lifeless, so ready to die. The receptionist smiles at him sympathetically yet takes her time finding the room number.

He walks down the hall, a knot in his chest. Old people get sick. That's what they do. They get sick and then they die. He quickens his pace. Room 234. On the left. He knocks once. The door swings open. His wife is standing by the bed. She looks up. Tears are streaming down her face.

The doctor leaves the room, so that it is just the three of them. Chinhominey's eyes are partially open, so it looks like she is sleeping. But her lips are curved in a slight smile, so Yung Chul knows that she is not sleeping. Chinhominey never smiles when she sleeps. Yung Chul stands, still as a statue. Myung Hee brings him a chair, makes him sit. He looks up at her. His eyes are full of questions.

"Your mother complained all day that she had a headache. Then, as I was preparing dinner, she came into the kitchen. She looked pale. She had dark circles around her eyes, and she lacked energy. Suddenly, she bent over, clutching her stomach. She admitted that she had a stomachache since the last night. I decided to take her to the hospital.

"The doctors took X-rays. They asked her so many questions. They told her there was nothing wrong with her. But instead of being relieved at the good news, she told them they were wrong. That is when I called you. I told her you were coming, and that seemed to calm her. Then she did something that she has never done. She took my hand.

" 'Please forgive me,' she said, 'I am asking you to forgive me for the lies I told you.'

" 'What lies are you talking about?' I asked.

" 'The lies I told you. About your marriage. About your children. The Fortune Teller never told me that your marriage was ill-fated. She never told me that your second child would die young. I made that all up. You were right when you said that I was envious of your love. I was afraid. I was afraid of being left alone. But my lies left me alone anyway.'

"It was almost more terrible to hear her confession than it was to have suffered from her predictions. She looked me in the eyes. She no longer looked pale and weak. Her eyes were brilliant and flashing. She clutched my hand tightly. She looked very strong, but not angry. She was smiling.

"She said, 'I want you to know that your fate has not been determined. Your marriage is not doomed. Your children's lives have not been decided. They have not even been lived! You cannot blame the heavens any longer. You can change your lives. It has not been decided!'

"And then she closed her eyes and lay back on the pillow, as if those last words had robbed her of all her energy. She had such a peaceful expression I thought Chinhominey was only resting."

•

Chapter 29

The Golden Gate Bridge looms ahead, breathtaking in its perfection, truly golden in the warmth of the setting sun. But as Grace drives closer, her spirits nosedive. The beauty of the bridge puts her own failures in sharp relief. Other human beings accomplish things. They build magnificent bridges, palaces, sculptures. Whereas she, she can't even get into law school. She can't even find someone to love.

Yet, the city seems to welcome her. The lights illuminate parts of the skyline. She makes her way safely across the bridge and finds a space in the parking lot overlooking the San Francisco Bay where several tourists shivering in shorts hurry back to their buses. They remind her that she is cold, that she is wearing jeans and a thin blouse. A couple of joggers run past, their faces red with exertion, panting like dogs, their eyes glazed in endorphin-induced euphoria. Grace continues walking toward the bridge. A woman is closing up her souvenir stand. The wind blows harder. Grace shivers, the skin on her arms stands out in angry bumps. She wraps her arms around herself and walks on, her hair whipping around her face, making it hard for her to see along the narrow pathway, making way for other pedestrians. The bay seems to stretch forever. The water glistens in the fading sunlight.

Leaning over the railing, she stares into the water that beckons to her from below, reflecting the early evening sunlight. At the horizon, the sun is a brilliant red arc that slips further and further into the sky, until finally, in the blink of an eye, it disappears. A shadow falls across the city. Nothing to stop the night from creeping across the sky.

The water shimmers. It doesn't seem that it would hurt, to fall into the water. She imagines that it would be like falling into a vat of cool, bouncy jello, blue jello, black jello. She imagines it would be like falling into warm, welcoming arms. But of course it wouldn't, it would be as deceptive as falling in snow. The first time she went skiing, she thought that falling in snow would feel like falling on a pile of soft cotton. But she was wrong. The snow was hard as cement. Hard and cold.

The water would be cold, too. Cold and unforgiving. But maybe beneath the black, shimmering water, it would be warm. Soft and warm, like a down blanket, like an embrace, protecting her, comforting her, pulling her in, pulling her down, down under. Perhaps after the initial impact, after the shock of the fall and the cold water, when she started to sink, wouldn't it be warm, then?

There have been many suicides on the bridge. So many people are enamored with the idea, such a romantic way to go! Falling, falling, twirling in the wind, arms reaching out, spinning around, her hair would blow around her, and then she would land, straight into the heart of the bay, past the hard, cold top layer, straight down, into the warmth of the deep black waters, rushing over her, swallowing her up.

Glug, glug, bubbles gurgling out of her nose and mouth, as she plummeted, straight down, to the bottom of the bay. Trapped underwater, a slow death, or trapped in mid-air, falling, the moment of suspension, of knowing that you were going to die but helpless, unable to do anything, either to save yourself or get it over with, end it quickly, being helpless, at the will of the gods who were not yet certain, had not yet chosen although it was clear what their decision ultimately would be.

She wipes her sweating palms against her jeans and grips the cold steel railing, tightly, so that she doesn't slip. And what if she changed her mind? Halfway down? What if she realized what a mistake she had made? What then? There would be nothing she could do. Conquer your fears. She leans the weight of her body on her hands and lifts herself up, so that her feet are dangling several inches off the ground. She looks out across the water, the water stretches forever. They would never find her. It would take days for her body to float to the surface. Suddenly, her sweaty hands lose their grip, slide across the cold metal. She falls to the ground, hitting her chin on the railing. The pain shakes her, awakens her from a daze. Her blouse is damp with perspiration. She tilts her head up, towards the sky. Her teeth chatter, making a clacking wooden sound. She is cold, her chin hurts, but her physical discomfort soothes her. *I'm alive. It's not going to be the end of the world.*

The woman at the souvenir stand is arranging pencils in a cup as Grace approaches her.

"We're closed," she says.

"I just wanted a pencil," Grace says.

The woman hesitates, looks Grace over, and relents. She hands Grace a pencil.

"Fifty cents."

Grace hands her two quarters.

"You know," the woman says, watching Grace with sharp, inquisitive eyes, "I saw you on the bridge. I was afraid that you were going to jump. I've been working here for twenty-seven years. You get a sense."

Grace holds the pencil in her hand, rolls it between her fingers.

"Have you ever seen anyone jump?" she asks.

"Once. I heard a scream. I looked out and saw this body falling through the air. Real slow. Like it was in slow motion," she pauses, remembering. "People still do it. I still hear the screams. Seems like halfway down, some people change their minds."

Chapter 30

The jar that contains Chinhominey's ashes is pure jade. Chinhominey brought the jar with her from Korea, perhaps intending to give it to Myung Hee as a gift. Yung Chul puts the jar on the mantel above the fireplace and the family pays its last respects.

Christina looks quickly at the jar as she hurries past. But her conscience beckons her back. Chinhominey, she thinks, who complained about housekeeping enough when she was alive, should not have her remains surrounded by dust. She retrieves a cloth and carefully wipes away the layer of dust that has gathered on the lid and on the mantel. She reaches up, feeling her dress bind her waist. She kisses the lid and places her cheek against the cool jade. She sheds a few tears for the old woman with the parasol, and wishes Chinhominey the peace she was unable to find during her lifetime. She wipes her tears from the lid and replaces the jar.

Grace, unlike Christina, is unable to walk past the jar without first stopping, staring at the green color that seems to fade in some places and deepen in others. She is fascinated, lured by the knowledge that it contains her grandmother's ashes. Her grandmother! Burnt to a crisp, she thinks, until she is now, nothing but flakes! She stares at the jar, hesitating, but her curiosity is uncontrollable. When she is sure that nobody is looking, she takes the jar off the shelf and removes the lid. Nothing but darkness. She shakes the jar to one side and a little bit of her grandmother flutters onto her hand. When Grace tries to remove the ash, it smears, leaving a black smudge on her wrist. She tries to wipe it off, but succeeds only in rubbing Chinhominey deeper.

Myung Hee pays her last respects after her husband and her children have left the house. She talks aloud to Chinhominey. She tells her about Grace, how she refuses to go to law school even though she was accepted by several of the top schools in the country (Not Harvard, but who cares? Myung Hee has heard that the law school's ranking was slipping anyway).

"She has the idea that she wants to be a psychologist," Myung Hee says to her mother-in-law, "She wants to go to Berkeley where crazy people walk around naked and smoke marijuana. It makes me worry."

For once, her mother-in-law is silent. No criticism, no complaints, no scolding. Myung Hee, encouraged by the lack of negative response, continues, "I worry that she will get hurt. What if she meets some crazy people? What if she starts to take drugs? What if she becomes involved with Communists?"

Chinhominey is receptive, quietly listening.

And then Myung Hee remembers. Her burden has been

lifted. She no longer needs to worry so much about Grace. Grace's destiny is her own to make. Still, it will be difficult not to worry about her daughters. She is, after all, still their mother.

She reaches for the jade jar, holds it in her hands, seized by a desire to have a last look. But there is no point in taking any chances. She replaces the jar without removing the lid. There is no point in tempting fate.

Yung Chul visits Chinhominey in the middle of the night when the rest of the family is asleep. He touches the jar, takes it off the shelf, and holds it in his hands. He sheds a few tears, and then a few more. He too thinks about taking the lid off the jar for one last look at his mother, but it seems disrespectful. He has a few faint stirrings of guilt. He had listened to his heart and disobeyed his mother's will. Still, he has no regrets.

She had tried so desperately to prevent the inevitable. She had stooped to deceit, telling him that his marriage was doomed! And why? So that he would fulfill his obligations as an only child, as her son. She had held on so tightly that he had to escape in order to avoid suffocation. But she forgave him, in the end, for his abandonment, for forsaking his filial duties. It is his turn now. And already he is forgiving. Already, Chinhominey is forgiven.

He puts the jar back on the mantel. Then, he walks upstairs and climbs back into bed, next to his wife, his beautiful wife, who is no longer pretending to be asleep.

Epilogue

It's strange to be back home.

It has been seven months since she moved to Berkeley. Grace pushes open the front door. She can hear her parents banging pots in the kitchen, cooking dinner. Her mother is singing a song whose lyrics she does not recognize for they are Korean. Somewhere, a baby is crying. Jung Soo must be three months old, Grace guesses.

Grace walks quietly upstairs. Christina, her hair wrapped in a towel, is walking naked around the room, cradling her baby in her arms. She has gained some weight and looks healthy, smiling as she tickles the baby's nose with her finger.

Christina looks up and sees Grace. Her smile widens. "Say hello to Aunt Gracie," Christina says, waving her baby's arm at Grace.

"He's so cute, and so small," Grace says, amazed, "I . . . I didn't expect him to be so tiny."

"He's only four and a half months. Jung Soo Choi." Christina nuzzles her son and asks, "Could you hold him a minute? So I can get dressed?"

Grace takes the baby, reluctantly at first, afraid of dropping him. Awkwardly, she shifts Jung Soo in her arms. She finally holds the baby against her chest, laying his head against her shoulder. He makes baby noises in her ear and sucks on a lock of her hair. Grace kisses the top of his head. He is so cute! Grace decides that he takes after his mother.

"So how is your program?" Christina asks as she pulls on a pair of underpants. "How long before you're a doctor of psychology?"

"Seven years."

"You're dating someone, aren't you?" Christina asks slyly. Grace hugs Jung Soo closer. Jung Soo smiles and makes a gurgling noise like a pot bubbling over. Saliva seeps out of his mouth.

"I knew it!" Christina laughs.

"I like your hair that way," Grace says. Christina's hair has been cut to just below her chin.

"After the baby was born, I found it was too much trouble to blow dry it. I don't have time to fuss with my hair the way I used to," she says happily. "Since the baby, I don't have time to do much of anything but change diapers and go to work."

She flicks a comb through her hair. "What's the new guy's name?"

"Luigi," Grace says.

"Italian?"

Grace nods, "He's in my program. My therapist says . . ."

"You're seeing a therapist?"

"I thought it might be helpful," Grace says. "Anyway, he thinks it was definitely a good idea to move away from home. You know, go someplace where nobody would have any preconceptions."

After a moment, Christina asks, "How old is he?"

"I don't know. About 50."

"You're kidding?" Christina asks, shocked, "You're dating a 50-year old?"

Grace laughs, "No. I was talking about my therapist."

"Well *I* was talking about your boyfriend."

"He's not my boyfriend, yet," Grace says good-naturedly. "He's older. Thirty-one."

"Thirty-one," Christina says, "That's a good age."

Grace notices how wistful her sister sounds, guesses that Henry is thirty-one. Jung Soo starts to cry. Christina holds out her arms.

"My baby, please," she says.

Back in his mother's arms, Jung Soo stops crying immediately.

It is a Korean custom to remember the dearly departed on special occasions. New Year's Day, birthdays and, of course, the anniversary of the day of death. Grace has come home to celebrate the first anniversary of Chinhominey's death. Myung Hee has prepared Chinhominey's favorite dishes and placed a large, flattering framed picture of the guest of honor at one end of the dining table.

The Choi family gathers around the table, and each member pays his or her respects by bowing down before the picture three times. A pair of chopsticks is placed first in the rice bowl then in each of the special dishes, so that Chinhominey's spirit may enjoy the meal. The family stands behind their chairs, watching as steam rises from a bowl of rice and each of seven prepared dishes — *chap chae, jun, pae jun, mandoo, chige, pindaduk,* and *bulgogi.* Chinhominey smiles at them from the photograph propped against one of the chairs. She seems to be enjoying the meal. Myung Hee passes the chopsticks from one dish to the next.

Finally, Chinhominey is finished. The family sits down to dinner.

Myung Hee starts cutting food into little pieces for Christina who protests that Amma, I can chew food, *I'm* not the baby!

"Hey grandmother," Yung Chul says, "What about me? How about feeding your husband?"

"You have two hands. And you still have most of your teeth," she says. "Feed yourself."

Yung Chul smiles sheepishly. Myung Hee looks lovingly at Jung Soo who is lying in his baby chair, smiling at nothing.

"What a nice looking baby," she says. "So handsome. A very intelligent face. A nice round head. An intelligent head, big enough to hold his brains."

Her husband nods.

"A very intelligent head," he concurs.

"He will grow up to be so handsome. A playboy," Myung Hee says. "And intelligent. A doctor."

"*Not* a doctor," Christina says, firmly.

"No, not a doctor," her father agrees.

"Okay, then a lawyer," her mother replies, "Later, a judge. A famous judge."

Suddenly, she puckers her lips, draws her eyebrows together in an expression of exaggerated concern.

"Husband," she says, alarmed, "Do you notice his ears?"

Yung Chul peers at his grandson's ears.

"He has nice ears," he says. "Nice, big ears. Good fortune."

"No," Myung Hee says, annoyed. "They are big but they are pressed against his head. He won't listen good to his mother. Or to his wife." She abruptly stands, picks Jung Soo out of his high chairs and walks out of the room. As she brushes past him, Yung Chul can smell the rich floral scent of his wife's perfume. It is from the bottle that he bought for her last Christmas.

Myung Hee walks back into the room. She returns Jung Soo to his baby chair. A cotton ball has been propped behind each ear, pushing it up and away from his head.

"Amma!" Christina complains.

Her mother scolds, "You'll thank me later when he grows up to be a good son. Very obedient. He will listen to you good."

Jung Soo starts to cry.

"Ssssh . . . ssshhh," Myung Hee says, picking up her grandson and handing him to Christina. The baby reaches out with his hands and smears sauce on his mother's new blouse but she doesn't notice, too engrossed in conversation.

Jung Soo catches sight of the photograph of Chinhominey. He stares at it, transfixed. Chinhominey returns his steady gaze. She has sacrificed a lifetime of good intentions for her gift to posterity, the gift of hope. Now she will be fondly remembered, not doomed to oblivion. After dinner, her photograph will join the family pictures on the end table in the living room, right next to Jung Soo's. Her great-grandson suddenly breaks into a delighted smile. Chinhominey smiles back. Her mission to America is accomplished.

Glossary

Anyonghasayo — formal way to say Hello.
bulgogi — Korean-style barbecue beef.
chap chae — silver sweet potato starch noodles stir fried in
  sesame oil with slivered vegetables and beef.
chige — spicy and hot (both in temperature and in flavor)
  Korean broth made from soybean paste and flavored with
  peppers, green onions, and often containing bits of cabbage
  and tofu.
Chinhominey — Korean word for paternal grandmother. The
  romanization for the accurate Korean pronunciation of the
  word would be "Chinhalmoney." The spelling of the word
  as "Chinhominey," however, is intended to reflect the
  Americanized way it would be pronounced by Grace and
  Christina.
daikon dahty — daikon is a large radish shaped like a tree
  trunk. Daikon dahty is a derogatory term for daikon-
  shaped legs.
dok guk — rice ovalette soup.
guitchana — bothersome, aggravating.
jun — fish fried in egg batter.
kalbi — Korean-style barbecued short ribs.
kim bap — rice, pickled radish, and barbecued beef rolled up in
  sheets of dried black seaweed.
kimchee — spicy pickled cabbage.
mandoo — Korean-style dumpling
pah jun — green onion fried in egg batter.

pindaduk — mung bean pancake flavored with leek, kimchee, and pork.

shikae — sweet beverage, best served chilled, made from rice water and sugar.

Uhmahnee — Korean word for "mother."

Uhmuhnim — polite yet intimate form of address for an older woman.